# clearwater crossing

# Just Friends

## laura peyton roberts

BANTAM BOOKS
NEW YORK • TORONTO • LONDON • SYDNEY • AUCKLAND

RL 5.8, age 12 and up
JUST FRIENDS
A Bantam Book/October 1998

ISBN 0-553-49258-6

Published simultaneously in the United States and Canada.

Bantam Books are published by Bantam Books, a division of Bantam
Doubleday Dell Publishing Group, Inc. Its trademark, consisting of the
words "Bantam Books" and the portrayal of a rooster, is Registered in
U.S. Patent and Trademark Office and in other countries. Marca Reg-
istrada. Bantam Books, 1540 Broadway, New York, New York 10036.

PRINTED IN THE UNITED STATES OF AMERICA

OPM   10 9 8 7 6 5 4 3 2 1

*For Rosie*

With sincere thanks to
Dean Rosenberg, Abaris Technologies,
and Andrew Klotz, D.V.M.,
for their generous assistance

If one falls down, his friend can help him up.
But pity the man who falls and has no one to
help him up!

Ecclesiastes 4:10

# *One*

"Excuse me?" Jenna Conrad said weakly.

She stared up at him from the driver's seat, her face completely expressionless in the glow from the dome light overhead, and Ben Pipkin could feel himself starting to sweat. Ben was still dressed as a werewolf from the haunted house fund-raiser Eight Prime had just wrapped up, and the perspiration rising under the brown greasepaint and patches of fake fur on his cheeks itched almost unbearably. From the pavement next to Jenna's mom's station wagon, he gripped the top of her open car door harder and took a deep, bracing breath of the cold night air.

"I'd really like to take you to the homecoming dance," he repeated, doing his best to sound confident. "I think we'd have a lot of fun."

He put his elbow on top of the door he held and leaned into the metal edge, striking a casual pose. Unfortunately, his angle was bad. The added weight on the door caused it to swing shut unexpectedly, nearly yanking him off his feet. He managed to extract his fingers a split second before they would have been crushed to pulp. Then, feeling incredibly thankful that all Jenna's body parts had been safely inside, he recovered his balance and sheepishly reopened the door.

"So, what do you say?" he asked, so unnerved by his own clumsiness that his voice cracked on the question.

Jenna regarded him with wide blue eyes. One finger twisted a strand of her long brown hair.

"It's just . . . well . . . I'm going with Peter," she said at last. "We always go to dances together. Thanks, though, Ben. It was nice of you to ask me."

"Oh." He let go of the car door and took a step backward, away from the light spilling onto the street. "Right. I guess I should have thought of that." Jenna did practically everything with her best friend, Peter.

"No. How could you have known?" she said, her voice conciliatory. "I'm sorry. I know this must be embarrassing."

"Embarrassing?" Ben squeaked. "No. Why?" *Mortifying* would have been a better word. "I mean, we're still friends, right? This doesn't change anything."

"Right," said Jenna, smiling. "Of course we are."

Even so, it was a very awkward moment. Ben had never asked a girl out before, and all the selfpsyching he'd had to do to find the courage this time wasn't paying off the way he'd imagined. He stood there staring at Jenna . . . she sat looking questioningly at him. . . .

*She's waiting for me to say good-bye so she can leave*, he realized suddenly. *What an idiot I am!*

"Okay! Well, that's good," he said quickly. "I guess I'll, uh, see you tomorrow, right?" Eight Prime was supposed to meet Sunday afternoon to clean out the ComAm warehouse, where they'd held their haunted house.

"Yeah, tomorrow."

Jenna waved from behind the closed window as he pushed her car door shut. A moment later she made a U-turn in the deserted street and headed off toward home. Ben stood in the middle of the pavement, waving with both arms over his head as her taillights receded into the darkness. When they were nothing but little red pinpricks, he finally breathed again.

"You *jerk*," he muttered under his breath. "What were you thinking, anyway?" He wandered off the edge of the road and plopped down on a boulder, his greasepaint-coated face in his hands. "How stupid can you be?"

With hundreds of girls at school to choose from, he'd had to ask someone in Eight Prime to be his date for the homecoming dance. He should have realized it was going to backfire—and that a rejection from one of his new friends would be far worse than one from a stranger.

*The problem is, a stranger would have said no for sure,* he thought miserably. *I don't exactly sweep women off their feet—not unless I knock them down, that is.* Ben knew the whole school thought him a hopeless nerd. He was an outcast, but he wasn't an idiot.

*No, wait. I am,* he reminded himself, depressed. *Just not that type of idiot.* His head sank further into his hands.

He never should have mentioned the dance to Jenna, let alone have asked her to it. Now, whenever they were around each other, he was always going to be wondering if she was thinking about what a fool he'd made of himself. And the worst part was, he didn't even have a crush on her. She was just a nice person—too nice to tell him no, he'd hoped. Now she probably thought he was madly in love with her or something. Ben groaned to imagine what she would tell Peter.

The sound of an approaching car made him raise his head. His father was coming to pick him up, but this car turned off at a corner far up the street.

He sighed. At least Jenna had said they were still friends. Actually, she'd seemed almost as eager to forget the whole thing as he was.

*I'm probably worrying about nothing,* he thought.

*Jenna's too nice to make a big deal about something like this—that's why you decided to ask her in the first place, remember? Buck up, already. Be a man.*

But he didn't feel like a man. He felt like a stupid little kid. No matter how hard he tried, he was always messing up, always doing something dumb. Just once in his life, he'd wanted to fit in. He'd thought that joining Eight Prime would be a big step in that direction, but ultimately it hadn't made much difference. The other members were usually nice to him, when they were together, but they all had separate lives. Unless there was a meeting or a fund-raiser, they pretty much ignored him.

And Ben wanted a separate life too. He wanted to be accepted by the other students at Clearwater Crossing High School. He wanted to get a date and have fun at a dance, like any normal person. He wanted people to say hello to him in the halls or invite him to sit with them at lunch.

It didn't seem like much to ask. And for a few days, in the flush of accomplishment he'd felt at the success of "his" haunted house, he'd been foolish enough to believe it was possible.

"I'm always such an idiot," he sighed. "No wonder no one likes me."

"Wow," Melanie Andrews said softly, leaning back into the passenger seat. "I didn't know I was going to do that."

5

Peter smiled slightly. "I can't say I was expecting it, either."

Blood whooshed in Melanie's ears with every beat of her heart. She had just kissed Peter Altmann!

One minute they'd simply been talking in his car behind the dark ComAm warehouse, and the next thing she knew, she had him in a lip lock. It had been all her doing, too. Peter had never moved.

"I—I'm sorry," she stammered, embarrassed.

Peter's smile widened. "That bad, huh?"

*No. Not bad. Not bad at all.* The thing was . . . she wasn't sure . . . had Peter been into it or not? He'd kissed her back toward the end, but he hadn't tried to stop her when she'd ended it. He hadn't put his arms around her and pulled her closer. And now, when any other guy would be trying to press the advantage she'd just given him, Peter sat regarding her calmly, a slightly amused expression on his face.

"I just . . . don't think I should have done that," she said, in spite of the fact that her entire body was still tingling.

Peter put a warm hand over hers. "Listen, Melanie, the truth is, I don't know what to think either. But we're friends, right? And that's not going to change—no matter how we feel about this tomorrow."

Melanie took a deep breath. "Yeah. You're right."

After all, it was just one kiss. It didn't have to be some major turning point between them. It didn't have to be anything at all.

"Well, I guess I'd better take you home."

Peter twisted the key in his Toyota's ignition, and the engine came to life, shattering the silent Halloween night. Melanie snuck peeks at his profile as he drove out from behind the ComAm building onto the deserted road. His dark blond hair was short on the sides, but the longer hair on top had a tendency to fall over his blue eyes, the way it was doing now. His nose was straight, his jawline strong. But the best part of all was his smile—open and friendly, with perfect white teeth. When Peter smiled, Melanie felt it in her gut.

She wanted to say something now, as they cruised the quiet streets, but she found herself at a loss. Everything she thought of seemed so superficial, such an obvious smoke screen to cover what had just happened. She didn't want to talk simply for the sake of diverting attention to another subject. Peter wasn't doing that, and she wouldn't do it either.

*On the other hand, what do you say to a guy you've just kissed for no apparent reason?*

"Would you want to go to the homecoming dance with me?" she blurted out as the car rolled up to a stoplight. "I mean, you don't have to. I'll definitely understand if you think it's too weird. But,

7

well, I have to go with someone, and I'd really like it to be you."

The light turned green, but Peter didn't drive forward. It didn't matter; no one was behind them at that late hour.

"Me? Are you sure?" he asked. "There are probably a hundred guys at school who'd kill to go to that dance with you."

"But you aren't one of them," Melanie said, dropping her gaze. She was sure her cheeks must be red even in the half-light of the intersection.

"I didn't say that." Peter pushed his bangs off his face. "I just don't want you to feel like you *have* to ask me or something. I mean, you know, after what just—"

"No. I want to," Melanie interrupted. "I've been thinking about it for a while, actually. It was just that, before, I thought you might be taking Jenna. But now that you've said there's nothing romantic between you . . ." She let the sentence dangle. She wasn't going to beg.

Peter hesitated only a second. "All right. I'd like to go with you. But how is this going to work, exactly? I mean, are you picking me up and bringing me a corsage, or will that still be my job?"

Melanie looked up to see a wide, teasing smile on his face.

"Very funny," she said, slapping his arm playfully.

"And by the way, that's the second time that light's turned green."

Peter glanced at the traffic signal, then put the car in gear and drove. "No, really," he said, still smiling. "I don't want to wear a corsage."

"You goof." Melanie could feel her own happy grin spreading from ear to ear. "I was going to get you a really nice one, too."

Jenna risked a glance at the ornate iron bench where she usually met up with Peter after Sunday-morning services. He was in the middle of a big crowd congratulating him on the success of Eight Prime's haunted house. Adult members of the congregation had volunteered as chaperones, and Jenna imagined they were asking how much money had been made and what the next fund-raiser would be.

"Why aren't you over there with Peter?" Jenna's mother asked, interrupting her own conversation with two members of the choir. "Don't you want to say hello?"

She didn't, actually. Not after the fight they'd had the night before. Or that she'd had, anyway. She wasn't too sure now whether Peter had been in on it or not.

"Jenna and Peter are *fighting!*" her younger sister Maggie sang, her head of auburn curls conspiratorially close to Allison's blond one.

The pair giggled as if Maggie were a comic genius, and Jenna felt her temper rising. Ever since those two had moved into the same room together, their annoyance factor had gone up by far more than the expected multiple of two. Of the six siblings in the Conrad family, Jenna was the third, after Mary Beth and Caitlin. Maggie came after Jenna, Allison next, and ten-year-old Sarah last. Instead of behaving like the seventh- and eighth-graders they were, though, together Allison and Maggie acted younger than Sarah.

"We are not," Jenna said irritably. *Not right now, anyway.*

"Then why don't you prove it?" Allison taunted. "Why don't you walk on over there and give Peter a big, wet kiss?"

"Why don't you—" Jenna began, but her mother broke in before she could finish her suggestion.

"That's enough! Really, Allison, I thought you'd outgrown that type of thing."

"Jenna started it!"

"*Me?* I'm just standing here minding my own business! You ought to try it sometime, Allison."

"Stop it right now!" Mrs. Conrad's voice was low and embarrassed. "Have you all forgotten we're at church?" She glanced across the concrete pavement in front of the building to where Mr. Conrad and Sarah were talking to a group of men. "Why don't you girls go see if your father is almost ready? Or go wait in the van with Caitlin."

Maggie and Allison threw Jenna victorious glances, as if they'd somehow come out on top.

"I'm going to talk to Peter," Jenna said, walking off. Anything was better than hanging around Maggie and Allison. Besides, as much as she hated to bring it up just then, there was something she needed to ask him.

The crowd of adults had drifted off by the time she joined him. "Hi," she said warily.

"Hi." Peter smiled and motioned for her to sit beside him on the bench. "How are you?"

It was so like Peter to pretend nothing had happened the night before; she knew it was his way of telling her he'd already forgotten her immature little outburst. The problem was, Jenna didn't want him to forget it. How could he have chosen to drive Melanie to and from the haunted house instead of her? For that matter, how could he have spent all that time working with Melanie when he could have been working with her? Just thinking about it made her nearly ready to argue with him all over again.

Still . . . Halloween was behind them now. And she had to get this homecoming thing straightened out.

"I'm fine," she said, attempting to smile. "You?"

11

Peter nodded. "Fine."

"Good." And then everything came out in a rush. "Listen, Peter, I need to make sure we're going to the homecoming dance together. I mean, I assume we are, and that's what I told Ben, but normally you'd have said something by now, and I can't stand it that you're waiting until the last minute when you know I have to ask my parents and get a dress and—"

"Whoa! Wait a minute," Peter interrupted. "You assumed we were going together?"

Jenna looked into his confused blue eyes and felt her stomach drop. "Shouldn't I have?"

"I think maybe you might have asked me."

"I was expecting *you* to ask *me*."

Peter shook his head. "You should have let me know. It's just . . . well, Melanie asked me last night and I said I'd go with her."

"*What?*" Jenna's angry voice turned heads outside the church. With an effort, she lowered it. "You said yes? Just like that? We always go to dances together."

"We used to. But I thought . . . I don't know. I mean, with Miguel and everything. . . . Well, things are changing, aren't they?"

"Miguel has nothing to do with this!" Jenna whispered furiously.

"Miguel has everything to do with this," Peter disagreed.

"So, what? Now you're punishing me for not

12

telling you I liked Miguel? Is that what this is about?"

"I didn't know you'd think it was punishment."

"How could you not?" Jenna demanded. "What do I have to do to make you understand? You spend all your time with Melanie lately and hardly any with me!"

"That's just not true."

Jenna wanted to scream that it was—it was, it was, it *was*!—but people were looking their way again. "Fine," she whispered back. "Then tell her you're going with me instead."

Peter made a face. "I can't do that."

"But I already told Ben that you and I were going together!"

"So? Why does Ben care?"

Too late, Jenna realized she hadn't explained that part very well. "Because he wanted me to go with him," she admitted reluctantly.

"But Jenna, that's perfect! Call him and tell him what happened and the four of us can all go together. It'll be fun."

"I doubt that's what Melanie had in mind," she said sourly. Not to mention what *she'd* had in mind. Jenna had known she wouldn't be going with Miguel, of course, but she'd thought she could at least count on Peter. To have her crush and her best friend *both* ditch her for other people seemed like the ultimate insult.

"No. Maybe you're right," Peter said slowly. "But you and Ben could meet us there. Why don't you?"

"Because I'm not going with Ben, that's why! I'm not going, period."

"Aw, don't be that way, Jenna. How was I supposed to know you—"

"I'll be however I want!" she retorted, jumping to her feet. "Have fun working with *Melanie* at the warehouse this afternoon." She stormed off across the parking lot.

"What's that supposed to mean?" he called at her back. "You're not coming to help clean up now?"

*I wish!* she thought. But she'd already promised Eight Prime she'd help take down the haunted house that day, and she'd keep her word. She didn't have to talk to Peter while she did it, though.

"You don't have to bring a date to the dance, you know," he shouted. "If you don't want to go with Ben, you could always go with a girlfriend."

Jenna turned around. "This isn't about Ben!" She opened the sliding side door of her father's blue van and climbed inside before Peter could reply.

Caitlin looked up from studying a hangnail as Jenna dropped into the backseat beside her. "Tough morning?" she asked quietly.

"You have no idea."

# Two

Nicole shivered as the afternoon shadows claimed the last bit of parking lot next to the gym. "Where are you, Jesse?" she muttered impatiently. After-school football practice was over and most of the other Wildcats had already driven out of the lot, but Jesse's conspicuous red BMW still crouched in its corner space, nearly the last car there.

*He's making it awfully hard to pretend I just happened to be walking through here*, she thought anxiously, looking at her watch. *Maybe I should tell him I missed my ride and came down to see if I could catch one with him. That might be more believable.*

On the other hand, it probably didn't matter what excuse she picked—she had a feeling he'd see through them all. Still, she couldn't exactly tell him the real reason she was there: *Hi, Jesse! I thought I'd waylay you here in the parking lot and try to talk you into asking me to the homecoming dance this Saturday.*

No, that definitely wasn't the way to go. Telling

him anything—telling him she was collecting leaves for a science project—would be better than that.

Nicole considered that possibility. *Hmm, not bad.* She was still trying to decide whether or not to grab a handful of leaves from the piles at the edge of the parking lot when Jesse came out of the gym.

He walked directly to his car, his head down and his eyes on the pavement. His brown hair was wet from the showers, and his shoulders looked wide and strong inside his green letterman's jacket. Nicole felt her pulse speed up the way it always did when she first caught sight of Jesse.

He reached the BMW and unlocked the driver's door, then swung the gym bag off his shoulder in one fluid movement. And even though Nicole had been waiting for that moment, it happened so fast she almost missed it. Jesse was starting his engine before she moved.

"Jesse!" she called out suddenly, running toward him across the pavement. "Hey, Jesse! Wait!"

He rolled down his window as she reached the car. "What do you want, Nicole?" he asked abruptly. He didn't seem particularly glad to see her.

"Well, I was, uh, down here, for, um . . . and I thought, uh . . . could you give me a ride home?"

A flash of irritation crossed his face. Then he shrugged. "Yeah, all right. Hop in."

Nicole sauntered around the front of the car, doing her best to look calm and carefree, but her hands were slick with sweat as she grabbed the metal door handle. She had counted on Jesse's being in a great mood that Monday. After all, it was Spirit Week and he'd just finished his first practice back with the Wildcats. But, strangely enough, he didn't seem the least bit happy. With a sinking feeling, Nicole dropped into his black leather passenger seat.

"So what happened to your ride?" Jesse asked as he sped out of the parking lot. "Courtney ditch you for Jeff again?"

"Um, yeah," said Nicole. Why hadn't she thought of that? Her best friend was always flaking out on her lately to spend time with her boyfriend. "How was practice?" she asked.

Jesse shot her a disgusted look. "It sucked. I don't even know if I'm going tomorrow." The BMW's tires squealed as he turned the corner onto the main road.

"Not going!" Nicole exclaimed. "But Jesse, you just got back on the team!"

"I'm not on the team, Nicole," he said grimly.

"But after you talked to Coach Davis last Friday, you said that—"

"I was deluded, all right?" His voice was loud and angry. "I thought if I got back on the field, it was as good as being on the team, but it's not. Do you know what that two-faced jerk did?"

17

She shook her head, afraid to speak.

"He gave Eric Spenser my position. Permanently! Even if he lets me play after homecoming, I won't be a starter anymore."

"What do you mean *if* he lets you?" Nicole dared to ask. "He has to let you."

"No, he doesn't. He made that crystal clear today." Jesse shook his head. "I don't even care anymore. There are only two more games after homecoming anyway."

*Only two more games and the state finals*, Nicole thought. But she didn't say it. She knew it was only attitude talking when Jesse said he didn't care about football. Sometimes she thought football was all he cared about.

"You're a much better player than Eric Spenser," she ventured after a moment. "Maybe the coach is just trying to make a point. After he sees you play, he'll probably give you your position back."

She had no idea whether or not that was true, but it sounded good. And she wanted—no, *needed*—to say the right thing just then. If she expected Jesse to ask her to the dance, she had to convince him she understood the situation and was totally on his side. "Besides, Eric is only a sophomore and you're a junior."

"You think I don't know that?" Jesse nearly shouted. His hands squeezed the wheel until his knuckles turned white. "And Coach isn't giving me anything, Nicole! I *earned* that position! I worked for it!"

Nicole flinched, but recovered quickly. "Right. That's what I meant," she lied. "Who does he think he is?"

Jesse went on as if he hadn't even heard her. "I shouldn't have to earn it all over again. It's like I'm starting from zero."

"It's not fair!" Nicole put in, beginning to get the hang of it.

"You're darn right it's not fair! And Coach isn't the only one, either. Hank and the seniors are barely speaking to me."

"Then they're hypocrites," said Nicole. "They're no choirboys themselves."

"Nate Kilriley is just busting for a fight. I swear one day he'll push me too far. . . ."

"Nate Kilriley is a complete troll!" Nicole declared passionately. "I've never liked that guy!"

Jesse finally cracked a smile—just the barest glimmer. "Who does?"

"When we were in grade school, he ate a bug," Nicole ad-libbed.

"He ate a *bug*?" Jesse repeated, smiling in earnest. "What kind of bug?"

"Well, I . . . I don't know," she admitted. "But he must have, don't you think? Just look at the guy— he's totally the type."

Jesse rolled his eyes. "If we're going to make things up, I can do better than eating bugs."

"Maybe. But I made you smile."

For the first time since she'd gotten into the car, Jesse turned his head and looked at her—really *looked* at her. "Yeah," he said. "Thanks."

That one simple word made Nicole's spirits soar. She'd done it! She'd finally had a conversation with Jesse that hadn't ended with her looking like a fool. "No problem," she said happily.

But as the streets slipped by, Nicole's feeling of triumph gave way to renewed anxiety. If she was going to get him to ask her to the dance, she only had a couple more minutes.

"So, you are going back to practice tomorrow, aren't you, Jesse? You have to."

"I guess so," he admitted grudgingly.

"You know, the homecoming dance would be the perfect place to hang out with the other guys and put all this behind you."

Major setback. He was looking at her as if she were crazy . . . and they were almost to her house!

"I know it sounds weird, but think about it," she urged. "Everyone will be in a good mood, ready to party. If you showed up like nothing was the matter, with a date dressed to kill . . . well, that kind of thing impresses people." She glanced down at her carefully coordinated Spirit Week outfit of forest green cords and a green-and-gold-striped sweater, matching all the way down to her thumb rings, hoping to suggest that she could deliver on the fashion end of things.

But Jesse just shrugged and pulled into her driveway.

"So, who are you going with?" she blurted out desperately.

"I have no idea. Until now, I didn't even think I was going."

Nicole felt short of breath. "You mean I changed your mind?"

"Maybe. I'll have to think about it."

She knew she should get out of the car, but she was so close. . . .

"I haven't decided who I'm going with yet, either."

Jesse nodded impatiently. "All right. Well, I guess I'll see you at school tomorrow."

"Okay," she said, reluctantly opening the passenger door. "And don't forget the Eight Prime meeting tomorrow night."

Jesse nodded again and was gone. Nicole watched his car disappear, wondering whether she ought to buy a dress or not. The dance was only a few days away. It was getting really late for him to ask her.

*Which means it's also getting really late for him to ask anyone else,* she reassured herself, heading up her walkway. *Meanwhile, I could be ready on a day's notice—if I had something to wear.*

He was probably only a heartbeat away from asking her. He'd go home tonight; he'd think about it; he'd realize that practically everyone normal already had a date. And then he'd remember that she didn't.

Not yet, anyway.

Nicole smiled as she pushed her front door open. *I'll go shopping tomorrow after school,* she decided, knowing her mother would give her the money. *There's no way I'm showing up at that dance in a dress that's anything less than fabulous.*

*There's Peter!* Ben thought excitedly, spotting him and Melanie walking across the high school's front lawn after Monday classes. Melanie was wearing her cheerleading outfit for Spirit Week, and Peter had on a dark green coat. Ben almost called out the other boy's name, but then thought better of it and began running to catch up to them. He'd have to get closer if he wanted to ask about the final profits on the haunted house.

He had felt awkward about seeing Peter and Jenna at the ComAm clean-up party the afternoon before, but it had turned out fine. Neither of them had treated him any differently, and no one else even seemed to know about his little blunder with Jenna. By the time the group had finished cleaning the warehouse and moved on to counting the ticket money, Ben was already well on his way to putting the incident behind him.

And they had made a *lot* of money—over four thousand dollars! Peter had warned them, however, that there were still expenses to deduct from the total—the cost of items such as nails, paint, fabric, and costume accessories—before they'd know how much progress they'd made toward the bus they were saving to buy for the underprivileged kids in the Junior Explorers program. Unlike some of the other members of Eight Prime, Ben was in no hurry to buy the bus and disband the group, but he was interested in knowing their latest profits.

Ben slowed to a walk as he covered the last few yards to Peter and Melanie, who were talking and laughing, intent on each other. They still hadn't seen him, so Ben crept silently up behind them, planning to surprise them good. But as he opened his mouth to shout hello, the words he overheard stopped him short.

"So what time are you picking me up for the dance?" Melanie asked Peter. "Seven o'clock?"

Peter shook his head. "That's too late. You have to at least let me take you to dinner first."

Melanie smiled. "Six, then?"

What was this? Peter was taking *Melanie* to the homecoming dance, not Jenna? Ben froze in his spot on the grass as the couple walked away, still oblivious to his presence. Then he turned and ran in the opposite direction.

*Jenna lied to me,* he thought miserably. It didn't

seem possible, but he'd just heard it with his own ears. *She lied to get out of going to the dance with a nerd like me.* Feeling so low he barely knew what he was doing, Ben changed course again and headed for the bus stop. *I really thought she was different.*

Jenna had always seemed so nice—too kind to judge a guy strictly by appearances—but even she didn't want to be seen with him.

His bus came and he boarded, ignoring the other students as he took a seat near the back. *I must be even more of a geek than I thought.* And that was saying something. He knew how low he ranked on the social scale—he wasn't blind.

Except without his glasses.

*These stupid glasses! I hate them!* Snatching them from his face, he glared at them with myopic eyes. It was bad enough that the lenses were thicker than submarine portholes, but he'd picked such a Poindexter frame! He should have known better than to get the exact same ones as his father, the software engineer. His dad was completely oblivious when it came to the outside world. He was so lost in writing his computer programs that his socks didn't match half the time. The guy wore a pocket protector, for crying out loud! No bigger geek had ever walked the planet Earth. *Yeah, and you're not even smart enough not to take his fashion advice.*

Ben could see it all now. His entire life loomed in front of him like a big-screen horror movie. If he didn't do something to change his image—and *fast*—he'd turn out just like his dad.

He shoved his glasses back onto his face as the bus stopped for a traffic light. Outside the window, a sea of black asphalt sprang into focus—the shopping mall parking lot.

"Wait! Wait, I'm getting out!" he shouted, jumping from his seat. He bolted up the aisle, somehow missing the feet that automatically stuck out to trip him, and stopped, breathless, beside the driver. "Could you let me out here?"

"This isn't a stop," Mr. Newman said dubiously. He was an enormously fat man, and the kids on the bus gave him correspondingly enormous grief. He seemed to think Ben was pulling some type of prank on him now, and he hesitated, one dimpled hand on the door lever.

"Light's green! Light's *green!*" a chorus of voices shouted.

"Please. I'm supposed to meet my mother here," Ben lied quickly. "I just remembered."

Mr. Newman gave him one last look, then shrugged and opened the door. Ben flew down the steps to the sidewalk, and the bus took off with a belch of diesel. Slowly he turned to face the enormous mall building. His spur-of-the-moment plan was desperate—even he knew that. But it was the only plan he had. He began jogging across the enormous parking lot.

Just inside the mall entrance was a small store-front branch of Ben's bank. Mr. Pipkin had commented on its presence any number of times. "Anyone who'd bank at the mall," he'd say with amusement, "really needs to reassess his savings plan."

But reassessing his savings plan was the last thing Ben wanted to do just then. Hurriedly, before he could change his mind, he scribbled his account number on a savings withdrawal slip and took it up to the teller.

"Six hundred dollars?" she asked, snapping her gum in time to the clacking keys of her terminal. "Are you sure? You've only got six-sixty in here. If you go below a hundred, you'll have to pay a fee."

"I have six hundred sixty-four dollars and forty-three cents," Ben corrected her. "Plus interest accruing from the first of the month. I'll pay the fee."

The teller replied with a single, spectacular snap of the pale pink wad in her mouth, then counted out the money. Minutes later, Ben was at the other end of the mall, stumbling in through the open glass doors of Sir Lens-a-Lot.

"I want contacts!" he announced loudly. A pair of customers looking over the glasses frames turned to stare at him with amusement. "I'm serious," he added desperately, like a man who was robbing a bank. "I want them, and I want them now."

A skinny young woman in an oversized lab coat

stepped out from behind the counter. "I'm sure we can help you," she said, pointing to a seat. "My father is with someone, but he's almost done. You can be next."

It was agony to wait his turn, but eventually it came. Sir Lens-a-Lot, whose real name turned out to be Dr. King, showed Ben into a tiny room full of equipment and eye charts. "May I see your glasses?" he asked, holding out his hand.

"You can *have* them." Ben handed the hated things over. "Once I get my contacts, I'm never wearing them again."

The doctor smiled as he used a machine to read Ben's prescription from the lenses. "You'd better hang on to them anyway. There's a breaking-in period before you can wear your new contacts all day. And there's always the possibility that you'll lose one. Or tear one. You're getting soft lenses, right?"

"Okay," Ben agreed, leaning forward in the patient chair.

The doctor loaded Ben's prescription into a machine that he pushed forward until Ben could peer through it, like some huge, weird set of binoculars. "Read the smallest line you can see clearly," he directed, pointing to an eye chart on the wall.

Ben read. Dr. King made an adjustment, and they repeated the process until the doctor was satisfied with the correction. Then they moved out of the room to the back of the store, where Ben sat in a regular chair by a counter. Dr. King selected two tiny, fluid-filled vials from a cabinet and peeled off their metal caps.

"Okay. This is the left one," he said, pouring the vial's contents into a shallow dish. Ben could just make out a barely blue circle against the white plastic. "We might have to try a couple to get a good fit, but let's start with this. Look directly at me. Now slightly up."

A moment later the doctor's fingertip was on his left eye, laying down a wet, gelatinous layer of plastic. Ben blinked and blinked as the finger withdrew. The contact didn't hurt—it just felt so *weird*. He squeezed his eye shut and a big, fake tear rolled down his cheek.

"How does that feel?" the doctor asked.

"Perfect," Ben answered without hesitation. "Great."

"Let me see you blink a few times."

"No problem." *Not* blinking—that would have been a problem.

The doctor watched the contact float around as Ben blinked on cue. "I think you're right. That looks pretty good to me. Ready for the other one?"

Through one eye the doctor looked fuzzy and through the other he was blurry. Ben thought he felt a headache coming on. "Yes. Absolutely," he said firmly.

In went the other lens. More blinking. More slimy fake tears. The doctor checked the fit, then handed Ben a tissue to wipe his face with. "Take a look out that way and see what you think," he said, pointing toward the front of the store.

Through the tears, Ben could make out the open door, and beyond that the mall. It was like some strange underwater scene at first, the images blurring and swimming in and out of focus. Gradually the picture cleared. There was still water around the edges and he was still blinking like crazy, but for the first time he could remember, he was actually seeing without glasses. "Not bad!" he breathed.

The doctor chuckled. "You're pretty nearsighted. It's always exciting for someone with as big a correction as yours. I'll show you the best part, though— something you've never seen before."

Dr. King pointed over Ben's shoulder and Ben turned his head to look. It was a mirror—a great big one—and right in the middle *was* a sight Ben had never seen before, a sight worth any price: his own face without glasses.

"Okay, then," said the doctor. "Let me tell you how to care for these and what the wear schedule is. Then we'll practice putting them in and taking them out a few times until you can do it yourself."

Ben nodded, but he was barely listening as the man ran through his instructions. Everything was printed on a handout anyway. Instead he practiced focusing—on the table, the doctor's face, the cabinet behind him. . . .

"Give it a try and see if you can do it," Dr. King's voice broke in.

"Huh?"

"See if you can take out the left lens and put it back in, the way I just explained."

"Oh. Right."

It was a little tricky at first, removing that limp glob of plastic, then getting it to hold its shape while he squirted it full of wetting solution and popped it into his blinking eye. Ben was determined, though, and with the doctor's encouragement, he got each of the lenses out and back in twice.

"All right, then," Dr. King finally said. "If you don't have any questions, you can pay up front. Liz will take your money."

Nearly two hundred dollars of his money, as it turned out, but Ben didn't care. He was so distracted he barely even noticed. In Sir Lens-a-Lot alone there were probably a dozen mirrors, not to mention that shiny place on the back of the steel cash register. He took his receipt and a plastic bag full of contact-care products from Liz in a daze.

"Good luck!" she called. "Enjoy them."

Ben nodded vaguely as he stepped into the mall. From every shiny vertical surface, his wide-eyed reflection stared back at him. Mirrors, windows, glass doors, and metal trim all reflected his cool new image.

Cool from the neck up, anyway.

Ben smiled as he blinked down at his wristwatch. It was still early enough. He still had plenty of money. . . .

"Maybe a leather jacket," he mused aloud. Leather was expensive, but with winter on the way, he'd be able to wear it all the time. Or maybe some sweaters. Or jeans. New shoes!

*Or how about all of the above?* he thought rebelliously. It would be like a holiday to shop for clothes without his mother hovering over him, contradicting his every decision.

"Oh, no, Benny," he could hear her say in his head. "Cotton is going to shrink and look wrinkly all the time. What you want is polyester." Or, "That's a nice look—for a delinquent." Or, "What in the world does a *boy* want with French cuffs? Come look at these cute striped T-shirts."

The all-time, hands-down winner, though, was the top-of-her-voice announcement she'd made one weekend in a packed Value-Mart. "Uh-uh. Not boxers, Benny. A growing boy needs briefs. Oh, look! The value pack has a free athletic supporter. See if you can find a small."

He loved his parents. He did. They were just so *embarrassing.* His father was such a nerd, and his mother was so overbearing and smothering and . . .

31

well . . . fat. Ben had known since Sunday school that he was supposed to honor his mother and father, not just love them, but he wasn't really sure what that meant. Not exactly. He was pretty sure it didn't mean he had to grow up to be just like them, though.

He squinted at the fancy department store at the end of the mall, feeling his new contacts move, then center, then move again with every blink of his eyes. They were driving him kind of batty, but it seemed a small price to pay, considering the alternative. *I'll get used to it,* he thought, beginning to walk.

In the meantime, he had a whole lot of shopping to do.

"Hi! Can I come in?" Caitlin asked after dinner on Monday, knocking on the frame of Jenna's open door.

"I wish you would." Jenna sat up on her bed and laid her Bible aside. "I was trying to read, but nothing's making sense to me tonight."

"Still mad at Peter?" Caitlin asked.

"Yeah." Jenna didn't ask her how she'd known. She supposed anyone with even average powers of observation could have figured that out if they'd been hanging around her as much as Caitlin had lately. "I was looking up everything I could find about friendship."

Caitlin smiled and sat down on the edge of the bed. " 'A man of many companions may come to ruin,' " she recited from memory, " 'but there is a friend who sticks closer than a brother.' That's a proverb."

"Really?" Jenna said, impressed.

Caitlin blushed slightly. "I guess I always liked that one because I never had many friends. But that verse seems to say that one real friend—one *true* friend—is all you need." She smiled. "When I was younger, I used to think that the friend in the verse was God. It made me happy to know he'd stick by me, even if no one else did."

"That's so nice!" It was easy to see how believing that could have comforted shy Caitlin.

"Yeah. I still like to think that sometimes. But my study Bible says it means a close human friend. Like you and Peter, maybe."

Jenna thought that over. "Maybe," she said slowly. There was a time not long ago when Peter had been closer to her than a brother. But now . . . lately it felt as if everything was unraveling.

"What did he do?" Caitlin asked.

"Who, Peter?" Jenna said, startled out of her thoughts. "Nothing. I mean . . . well . . . I'd tell you, Cat, but it's just too stupid. I'm embarrassed to even talk about it."

"Oh." Caitlin stiffened and half rose off the bed. "I'm sorry. I shouldn't have—"

"No!" Jenna cried, putting out a hand to stop her. "If I was going to tell anyone, I'd tell you. It's just kind of personal, that's all."

Caitlin didn't look convinced, but she did sit back down.

"So how's the dog?" Jenna asked to change the subject.

"She's doing great!" Caitlin answered, immediately more at ease. "Oh, she's so sweet, Jenna. In fact, I thought maybe you'd want to come down to the garage and see her."

"Why?" Jenna asked dubiously. The stray dog Caitlin had rescued at the ComAm warehouse was the mangiest creature Jenna had ever seen. She was glad that having it around made her sister happy, but the last thing she wanted was to get anywhere near it herself.

"She looks better every day. Dr. Campbell—the vet I took her to on Saturday—said I'm doing a great job with her. She comes when I call her, and she sits now too. She let me hold her all through the visit, even though Dr. Campbell had to give her a bunch of shots, and you could tell it really hurt when he cleaned out those abscesses on her hind legs. I did the best I could with those, but Dr. Campbell said they'd probably been infected a long time. He's really nice. He showed me how to give her antibiotic pills. You just open her mouth, like this, and then you stick the pill right down her throat." Caitlin demonstrated on the empty air in front of her. "When I hold her mouth closed, she has to swallow."

"That doesn't sound very safe. Can't you just hide the pill in food or something?"

Caitlin shook her head, a proud smile on her face. "Nope. Abby is way too smart for that. I tried it once, and when she got to the pill, she spit it right back out."

"*Abby?*" Jenna repeated loudly. "It has a name now? Caitlin, you know Mom isn't going to let you keep that dog."

"No, no. I know," Caitlin said, temporarily rattled back into shyness by her rare slip of the tongue. "But I have to call her something, don't I? Dr. Campbell said you have to give a dog a name in order to train it. It has to learn to respond to its name."

"But why are you bothering? Let the next person train it when you find it a new home."

Caitlin gave her a wounded look.

"I just don't want you to be hurt when you have to give it away, Cat," Jenna hurried to add. "And the more time you spend with it, the harder saying good-bye is going to be."

"The better trained she is, the better the home I can find her," Caitlin countered. "Besides, I can't even start looking until I take her back to Dr. Campbell on Wednesday. He's going to check those sores again."

"What is all this costing? Where are you getting the money?"

Caitlin absolutely beamed. "Dr. Campbell is the nicest man! Once he found out Abby was abandoned, he gave me huge discounts on everything. It hasn't cost much at all."

"That *is* nice," Jenna agreed cautiously. She couldn't believe how fired up Caitlin was over Dr. Campbell. The only thing harder than believing shy Caitlin had gone to consult this stranger by herself was imagining her actually talking to him.

"You can come with me on Wednesday, if you want," Caitlin offered. "I'm not going until the afternoon."

It was on the tip of Jenna's tongue to decline. She wasn't even sure why Caitlin would ask her on such a boring errand. But then she reconsidered.

*It's not like I'm going to be busy doing anything with Peter,* she remembered miserably. *I might as well go with Caitlin.*

Besides, she was kind of curious to meet the man who could turn her sister into such a motormouth.

# Three

When Melanie walked into the gym for practice on Tuesday afternoon, her seven fellow cheerleaders were lined up on the hardwood floor, facing a woman who could only be the squad's new coach. She was young—early twenties—and the lightweight red-and-white running suit she wore had an immaculately ironed crease precisely down the center of each leg and sleeve. Her shoulder-length black hair was gathered into a perfect ponytail, with small red clips keeping the bangs smooth and a crisp white bow contrasting with the dark brown skin of her neck. Her shoes were white too, and as spotless as if they had just come out of the box. Around her neck a shiny silver whistle hung from a scarlet cord.

"Hallelujah," Melanie murmured, hurrying to join the others.

"You must be Melanie," the woman said as Melanie took a place at the end of the line. "I'm your new coach. I was just explaining that the school wants you all to call me Ms. Kincaid, but I prefer Sandra—you'll just have to use your judgment. I graduated from Clearwater University this spring, where I was a cheerleader all four years. Plus in high school. And junior high."

"Hallelujah!" Melanie breathed again. This was getting better by the second.

Tanya stifled a giggle to her left and she and Melanie exchanged brief, meaningful glances. *No more kissing up to Vanessa!* the glints in their eyes said. *No more calisthenics for Coach Davis! Finally, a real coach who's a real cheerleader too!*

"All right, then." Sandra looked up and down the line. "From what I understand, you girls have been more or less on your own for some time. Well, those days are over. I'm in charge now, and I plan to stay in charge."

Melanie's smile was so big it hurt as she snuck a peek down the line at Vanessa. The squad captain's close-set eyes stared straight ahead, and the rest of her face was similarly lacking in expression. Someone who didn't know her might have guessed she was simply bored, but Melanie knew she was steaming. Even so, she couldn't say she was sorry to see an end to Vanessa's power.

"My way of doing things might seem strange at first," Sandra continued. "It might seem like starting over. But I promise you I know what I'm doing.

Give me a chance, and together we'll make CCHS the best squad in Missouri."

There was a murmur of unrestrained excitement from the girls.

"Red River will only *wish* they were so good," Sandra added.

Tiffany burst into applause. And even though Melanie guessed the gesture was a not-so-subtle jab at Vanessa, she and the other girls joined in.

"Will we—I mean us juniors and Melanie—go to cheerleading camp this summer?" Angela dared to ask.

Sandra smiled incredulously, crinkling up the skin at the corners of her dark brown eyes. "We've *got* to go to cheerleading camp—that's half the fun!"

Everyone started talking excitedly, and the line lost any semblance of order as the girls crowded together. Sandra clapped perfectly manicured hands to break it up.

"In the meantime," she reminded them, "we have lunchtime spirit rallies every day and a homecoming game on Friday."

She turned and punched the Play button of a boom box on the polished wooden floor. A familiar song began playing loudly.

"This is your music, right?" Sandra shouted over the tune. "So let's see what you've got!"

"Everybody sit down, okay?" Peter called. "We need to get started." The members of Eight Prime all took seats in Peter's living room.

Leah and Miguel hurried to grab spots on the couch. It was where they usually sat, but this was the first Eight Prime meeting since the two of them had gone public as a couple, and Leah had to admit it felt a little strange to be openly sitting with Miguel, his tan hand over hers. She turned her head to smile at him and he winked in return. At school they were an item too now—together every second, holding hands in the streamer-festooned hall. . . .

"Hey, Leah!" Ben said from Miguel's other side. "I like your sweater."

Like most of the group, she was still wearing her Spirit Week colors from school, including a sweater of soft, dark green cashmere. "Um, thanks," she said, hoping he wasn't fishing for her to return the clothing compliment. She could still barely look at him without cracking up.

Everyone else had already arrived at Peter's house when Ben rang the bell. Peter had opened the door, then turned around wearing one of the strangest expressions Leah had ever seen. But when she caught sight of Ben, Leah had felt her own lips press together while her eyes flew open wide. Ben was dressed from head to toe in black leather.

Black leather! Leah had watched as one by one the others noticed Ben's leather pants and biker jacket, then looked quickly away, various muscles in their faces straining against laughter.

Amazingly, Ben hadn't seemed to notice—possibly because he was blinking so frequently that he couldn't follow the action. Apparently he was wearing new contact lenses on top of everything else.

Leah had whirled around to hide her face, pretending to want a soda, only to find Melanie and Nicole already at the refreshment table.

"Is he kidding?" Nicole had half whispered, half giggled. "Didn't anyone tell him Halloween is over?"

"Shhh!" Leah had cautioned. "He'll hear you!"

"She'd be doing him a favor if he did," Melanie had murmured. "Can you imagine what would happen if he wore that getup to school?"

Leah's eyes had widened once more—this time in alarm. Now, looking at Ben on the other end of the couch, she hoped he at least had the good sense not to try that.

"Okay," Peter said again, calling the meeting to order. He was sitting on the love seat with Jenna, holding up a big sheet of paper. "This is the treasury report, showing all the money we've made since we formed Eight Prime."

He pointed to the first row of figures. "This is our car wash—three hundred and fifteen dollars. And this line is the pumpkin sale, showing our profit of eleven hundred and twenty-eight dollars."

Everyone looked at the chart and nodded.

"And finally the haunted house," Peter continued, pointing. "We took in four thousand, seven hundred and fifteen dollars at the door. But after we deduct our expenses for paint, fabric, costumes, hardware, and everything else, we're left with a profit of four thousand, three hundred and twelve dollars. Oh, and eighty-three cents."

"That's great!" Leah exclaimed, leaning forward on the sofa. "And so the total in our savings account is—"

"Five thousand, seven hundred and fifty-five dollars and eighty-three cents," Peter finished for her, his index finger on the bottom line.

The group broke into applause.

"And don't forget the interest!" Ben said. "We ought to be getting some interest on that money."

"You're right," Peter agreed, not looking at him. Leah suspected he couldn't, for fear of laughing. "I'll check on that and report it at the next meeting. I don't think it will be much, though."

"Still, that's almost six thousand dollars," Nicole said happily. "That's really good!"

"We must be at least halfway there," Jesse added. "I mean, we're buying a *used* bus, right? How much can it be?"

Jenna looked up from the steno pad she used to

record the meeting notes in. "Tell them about Mr. Haig," she urged Peter.

Leah suddenly realized that was the first thing Jenna had said all evening. *Strange*, she thought, *Jenna is usually pretty talkative*. But before she had time to think any further, Peter started talking again.

"Mr. Haig is a man at our church. He usually keeps to himself, but he has this sister who teaches at a fancy private school, and they have a bus they want to sell. Mr. Haig looked into it for us, and it sounds perfect! It's only five years old and hasn't been used a whole lot. The school bought the bus for field trips, but it's too small for most of their runs and they want to replace it with a larger one."

"How big is it?" asked Miguel. "Maybe it's not big enough for us, either."

"No, it's *perfect* for us," Peter told him. "The bus holds thirty-six passengers, which is enough for the kids, the counselors, and everyone's camping stuff too. We even have some room left over, in case Junior Explorers grows."

"So let's buy it!" said Nicole. "What's the problem?"

"They want twenty thousand dollars," Jenna told her.

"But it's worth twenty-four," Peter put in quickly. "That's what they'll be asking if we don't take it."

"Twenty grand!" Jesse exclaimed. "I *know* we can get one cheaper than that!"

"We can," Peter confirmed. "But Mr. Haig also looked at a couple of cheaper ones and said they were unreliable junk. We don't want another junky bus—not when we're driving little kids around. We vowed to buy the Junior Explorers a bus, and I think we meant a *good* bus, right? Don't forget we're donating it in Kurt's memory."

"Well, how do you know this Haig guy knows what he's looking at?" Jesse demanded. "Maybe he just wants us to buy his sister's bus."

Jenna shook her head. "He's a farmer, Jesse. And he not only takes care of the farm equipment on his own place, he fixes other people's too. My dad says he's probably the best mechanic in Clearwater Crossing."

Jesse rolled his eyes. "Which isn't saying much in this Podunk town," he grumbled.

Leah saw Melanie shoot him an exquisitely nasty look.

"I think we ought to buy it, then," Leah said, eager to head off another spat between those two. She turned to Peter. "If your friend recommends it, and Jenna's dad recommends *him*, then at least we know we're not being taken. It would be awful if we got something cheaper and it broke down on its first big trip. We'd have to start fund-raising all over again."

"That's what I think too," Peter said. "Better to spend the money up front than to spend it later on repairs."

"That would be fine—*if* we had the money," Nicole groused. "At twenty thousand dollars, we're not even halfway there."

"I know. You're right," Peter admitted.

There was a lengthy, rather depressed silence.

*Twenty thousand dollars—that means we still have over twelve thousand dollars to go*, Leah thought. She wasn't in as big a hurry to disband Eight Prime as Nicole and Jesse seemed to be, but she still found the numbers discouraging. *We'd have to hold three more events as successful as the haunted house to earn that*. And the haunted house had been so much work. . . .

"Why don't we take a week off and think about it?" Melanie suggested, breaking the silence at last. "The cheerleaders have to do stuff every day this week for Spirit Week, and I assume you're all going to the homecoming game and bonfire on Friday. Then Saturday's the dance." Leah wasn't sure why Melanie paused to smile at Peter. "Besides, we busted our butts on the haunted house, and we deserve a break."

"Hear, hear!" Nicole was quick to agree. "Let's worry about the bus next week."

Peter turned to Jenna. "How does that sound to you?"

She shrugged. "Okay."

"It can't hurt," Leah said. "We don't have the money for the bus anyway. A break gives everyone a chance to think, and maybe we'll come up with some great new way to raise cash."

"I'll even have the next meeting at my house," Melanie offered. "We can use the poolhouse."

"What day?" Biker Ben wanted to know.

Melanie looked at Peter again. "Thursday?"

"Good enough," Miguel answered for him, rising from the couch. "And that means we're done for tonight."

Leah stood up too, and a moment later everyone was saying good-bye. She and Miguel held hands as they walked through the darkness to his car.

"What was up with Ben and that ridiculous outfit?" Miguel chuckled in her ear. His lips were warm on her cold earlobe, and she snuggled against his side. "Man, I could barely keep from laughing."

Leah shook her head. "I know. Everyone was in the same boat."

"Where do you think he got it?" Miguel wondered aloud. "I mean, I've seen him wear weird things before, but those were just kind of nerd weird. This . . . this was *weird* weird."

"And what about the contacts?" Leah giggled. "He was blinking so often, I'm surprised he could see."

"He must not have been able to see the mirror.

Can you imagine what would happen if he ever tried that look at school?"

Leah didn't want to imagine. "I'm sure he wouldn't," she said quickly. But in her head she was remembering Melanie saying almost the exact same thing. Poor Ben. If he ever did go to school dressed like that . . .

*No. He wouldn't.*

Leah shuddered involuntarily. *Would he?*

"Jesse!" Nicole called out, running down Peter's front walkway to catch him after the meeting. "Hey, would you mind giving me a ride home?"

"Do you ever drive yourself anywhere?" he asked, but he opened the passenger door and motioned for her to get in.

Nicole took her seat without acknowledging his question. *If I'd driven myself, then I wouldn't have an excuse to ride with you,* she thought smugly, waiting for him to join her. The truth was that her lack of a vehicle that night had been very carefully planned—as carefully planned as the black crystal necklace and earrings she'd so painstakingly selected to go with the slinky red formal she'd bought that afternoon.

*Wait until Jesse gets a look at me in that dress,* she thought, smiling to herself as he started the car. *Melanie Andrews will be the last thing on his mind.*

"So how was practice today?" she asked.

He shrugged. "The same. I don't really want to talk about it."

That was okay. Neither did she. "I went to the mall after school and bought a dress for the homecoming dance," she volunteered.

"Uh-huh." His eyes were on the road, and his mind was obviously not on the subject.

Nicole tried again. "Have you rented a tuxedo yet?"

"What?" He threw her a baffled sideways glance, as if she'd just woken him up or something.

"Your tux for the dance. Yesterday you said you were going. You haven't changed your mind, have you?" Nicole's heart pounded as she waited for his answer.

"No. I guess not. I don't know," he said, annoyed. "The whole thing's such a pain in the butt. Renting a tux and finding a date . . . I don't know if it's worth the effort."

"But you have to go!" Nicole insisted. He was playing right into her hands. "It's going to be so much fun!"

"Yeah?" He raised one straight eyebrow and gazed at her with skeptical blue eyes. "So who's taking you?"

*Yes!* she thought. *Almost there. . . .*

"Well, I haven't decided yet. Homecoming's a pretty important dance."

Jesse laughed out loud. "Yeah, right. Don't you mean no one's asked you?"

"For your information, I've been asked plenty!" Nicole lied. "I'm just holding out for the right guy."

"Like who?"

*Like you!* she wanted to scream. Was he this dense with everyone or only around her?

"Well, I don't know. He'll have to be cute. And nice."

She paused. Nothing.

"He'll have to be someone I know," she continued. "I don't want to go with any random guy who asks me in the hall."

Jesse snorted. "That happens to you a lot?"

Nicole ignored him. "It would be nice if he asked me soon, too."

Jesse shook his head. "Well, with all those guys you have to pick from, I'm sure you'll find someone."

*This is not going the way I imagined,* she thought, frustrated.

"So who are you going with?" she asked, trying another tack. "I'll bet you don't know either."

Jesse rolled his eyes skyward. The gesture was so exaggerated that Nicole could see it even by the dim light of the dashboard controls. "I don't really care. I guess I'm not as picky as you are."

"That's good," Nicole told him, trying for sarcasm

in spite of her growing excitement. "Because chances are you won't have much to choose from."

Jesse smiled. "I'm not worried."

*He's just not going to take the hint*, Nicole realized. Meanwhile, she already had a dress—and quite an expensive dress at that.

She forced herself to count to ten, then drew a long, deep breath. "Listen, Jesse," she said slowly, working to keep her voice from wobbling, "I just had an idea. Since neither of us has a date yet, why not go together? It could be fun."

Jesse laughed. "Thanks, but I don't need a pity date, Nicole."

"I didn't say you did. I just thought—"

"Oh, no!" he cut her off. "Is *that* what this whole thing's about? You've been wanting me to ask you all along?"

"No! I only thought—"

"Forget it, Nicole." His tone didn't leave any room to argue. "You and I are just friends."

# Four

Ben slunk down the outside aisle of the locker room, desperately hoping he was the only one there. The end-of-lunch bell hadn't sounded yet. Everything seemed pretty quiet. . . .

He tiptoed along as softly as he could in heavy motorcycle boots and fearfully poked his head around the final corner. All clear! With a sigh of relief, he rushed down the aisle to his P.E. locker and hurriedly spun the lock. He had to retrieve his gym clothes and get changed before the other guys came in, or there was no telling what they'd do to him.

*I'm such an idiot!* he told himself, glancing down at his black leather clothes in despair. *Why couldn't I have picked something normal?*

He'd thought maybe he'd seen a few stifled smiles at Peter's house the night before, when he'd debuted his new look, but no one had said anything. No one had told him he was making a complete fool of himself. He'd thought he could count on his new friends for that much, at least, but his new outfit had passed without a murmur. The only thing anyone had commented on at all was his contacts, and those comments had been favorable.

Unfortunately, things hadn't gone nearly so well at school.

All day long people had been pointing and laughing or saying mean things. After second period some tough guys had taken his backpack and made him chase them all over, mocking him the entire time. He'd had to beg before they gave it back, and even so he'd been late to third period, where his civics teacher had handed him his first-ever demerit slip. He'd spent lunchtime hiding in a bathroom stall, missing a Spirit Week rally in the quad, and now all he wanted was to get into his gym clothes fast—before the guys who already thought fifth period was the Ben Pipkin Abuse Hour showed up.

The lock clicked at its final stop. Ben yanked the door open and grabbed his sweats and sneakers. He was about to put his backpack inside when he changed his mind and swung it up onto the bench beside him.

The first thing he had to do was take out his contacts. Instead of being nice and wet, the way they'd been that morning, the lenses had gradually turned gooey, then gummy, then dry, and now they were driving him crazy. It was time to switch back to glasses. Extracting his contact case from his pack,

Ben popped the little doors open and carefully removed his lenses, putting first one then the other to bed in their wetting solution. It felt so good to get them out! He paused to rub his irritated eyes a moment before he snapped the case shut and dropped it back into his pack, where he began fishing for his glasses.

"What have we got here?" a voice sneered behind him. Almost simultaneously, the end-of-lunch bell rang.

Ben froze, his empty hand still in his backpack. The voice belonged to Mitch Powell, the biggest bully in gym class.

"Geez, Pipkin," Mitch went on loudly. "I knew you were a loser, but I didn't know you were a homo, too."

"Yeah, he's a little leather boy!" another voice said with a nasty laugh. Ben's heart started pounding. There were two of them—Powell and his favorite sidekick, Whitey Wallace.

"Just leave me alone," Ben managed, feeling for his glasses again, but in an instant his backpack was yanked from his hands. He squinted up at the blurred shape of Mitch.

"What's a tough guy like you carry with him?" Mitch taunted, holding the pack over his head. "You got a gun in here, Pipkin? Maybe some brass knuckles to kick my butt with?"

Whitey laughed again—the mean, vacant laugh

of someone too lazy to think for himself. "Yeah, Mitch. I'll bet Pimple wants to take you on." A hand slapped Ben's head from behind, snapping his neck forward. "Isn't that right, Pimple?"

"I only want my glasses," Ben said, being careful not to whine. He'd learned the hard way that whining was an invitation to violence. "Just let me have my backpack." He stretched a hand toward Mitch, but didn't rise from the bench. It was easier to attack a guy when he was standing up—he'd learned that the hard way too.

Mitch smiled sadistically and took a few steps backward. Without his glasses, Ben could no longer make out his tormentor's face. "Come and get it, Pimple," Mitch urged, sitting down on the far end of the bench. Slowly, malevolently, he opened the backpack's double zippers wide.

Ben didn't need to see to know that in a few more seconds his belongings were going to be strewn all over the concrete floor, but being half blind put him even more at Mitch's mercy than usual. And Whitey was still lurking behind him, waiting to tackle him the moment he stood up.

Ben slid a few feet along the bench, his hand stretched out to Mitch. "Come on, Mitch," he pleaded.

Mitch reached into the pack and pulled out something white.

*My wetting solution!* Ben thought in a panic.

*What if Mitch dumps out my contacts? They'll be ru-
ined!* Even though most of the money he'd spent on
his new look had been wasted, Ben still had hope
for the contacts.

"You want this?" Mitch asked. Ben didn't move.
"No?" Mitch tossed the plastic bottle back over his
shoulder. It bounced off the bank of metal lockers
with a bang, then fell to the concrete floor. Ben
imagined the bottle split open, its contents leaking,
but he didn't dare retrieve it.

A flash of movement in the aisle behind Mitch
caught Ben's myopic eyes. He couldn't make out
who they were, but other guys were arriving. Ben
sighed with relief. No one ever interceded on his
behalf, but at least he wouldn't be beaten up now.
Mitch and Whitey were too cowardly to do anything extreme in front of witnesses.

Mitch's hand dipped into his pack again, and this
time Ben dared to dart forward, managing to get
one hand on a strap. "Let go!" he said in a shaking
voice.

"Ooh! Let *go*!" Whitey mocked him.

"Why don't you make me?" Mitch said. He held
the backpack with one hand and pulled out a
heavy civics book with the other. "Want this?" he
taunted. Then he flung it over his shoulder.

"Ouch!" someone barked. "Who the hell just
threw that? I swear to God I'll pound the living—"

"Me! It was me!" Ben cried, recognizing Beau

Kemp's unusually deep voice. Beau was the biggest guy in class by thirty or forty pounds, and even though he kept to himself, the other guys all feared him.

An amazed smile spread over Mitch's blurry features. "It's your funeral, sissy boy," he hissed, letting go of the pack and sauntering off. Whitey scurried along at his heels, equally reluctant to mess with Beau.

Ben plunged his hand into his pack, found his glasses, and put them on. When he looked up, Beau was towering over him, his ruddy face glowering.

"You honestly expect me to believe you threw this at me, Pipkin?" Beau said, holding out the textbook before he dropped it to the bench with a thud. "You're a whole lot of things, Pipkin—you're a piece of work and that's for sure—but I never thought you were stupid."

"I'm not stupid," Ben said quietly. "And I didn't throw it. I was just trying to get my stuff back from Powell." He was risking a lot on his assessment of Beau as a basically nice guy. He hoped he wasn't wrong.

"Powell threw it?" Beau demanded.

"You know if I tell you he'll beat me up later. I might as well just let you do the honors now."

Beau smiled a little. "Sorry, but I don't have time right now." He walked back to his open locker.

Ben hesitated only a second before he hurried

back to his own locker and rapidly began putting on his gym clothes. *I never should have tried to change my image*, he thought as he pulled on his sweats. *It just made me more of a target than before.*

He was used to the snickers, the condescending looks, the passive hostility of people who tried to trip him in the halls—and gym had never been a treat with guys like Whitey and Mitch around—but today things had turned really ugly. Ben wondered if Eight Prime had any idea how much he was picked on, how different his life at school was from theirs. If they did, they'd never mentioned it.

Not that he'd ever mentioned it either. He had that much pride, at least.

Ben flung his expensive black leather jacket into the locker, not bothering to hang it on the hook. *What a waste of money! What a stupid idea!* he thought, becoming angry with himself. He was old enough to know that clothes didn't matter, but he'd still wasted his entire life savings on a ridiculous outfit he'd never wear again. He stuffed his boots and backpack in on top of the jacket and slammed the door.

*I ought to just give up.* So what if he wasn't cool? Who cared if no one liked him?

*I care*, he admitted miserably. *I shouldn't, but I do.*

And besides, he knew what he would become— he'd turn out to be just like his father, the ultimate computer nerd. He had to do something if he didn't want to end up that way. But what? He didn't have a clue.

Ben sighed and bent to tie his gym shoes in the now-crowded locker room. *Oh well*, he thought, half resigned to his fate. *At least Dad is the best programmer in the Midwest. No one even cares what he looks like after they find out what a brain he is.* If he was destined to be a geek all his life, he hoped he'd at least be as brilliant a computer geek as his father.

*Hey! Wait a minute!* he thought.

And his eyes opened wide at the genius of his new plan.

Jenna barely knew what to make of Caitlin's strange behavior. As soon as they arrived at the vet's office Wednesday afternoon, Caitlin unloaded her stray dog from the back of their mother's station wagon and never looked back once. She didn't even glance behind her to see if Jenna was coming as she led it to the door. Inside, she ignored the fact that two other people were in the lobby and marched straight to the reception desk.

"Caitlin Conrad," she announced to the young woman sitting there. "I have an appointment with Dr. Campbell." Actually, she more whispered than announced it, but still. Jenna was amazed.

The woman, whose name tag said RHONDA, showed them into a room.

"I hope he doesn't find anything else wrong," Caitlin fretted while they waited. "Poor Abby." She lifted the dog onto the examination table and kissed its black nose. "You're a good girl, aren't you?" she cooed. "Yes, you're my poor good girl."

"Do you have to kiss its face?" Jenna asked, grossed out. "Who knows what kind of disease you'll catch that way?"

"People's mouths have more germs than dogs' have," Caitlin returned, unperturbed. "If you want to worry, worry about me giving something to her."

And then Dr. Campbell came in, wearing a bright green smock over his shirt and tie. "Hi there!" he said when he caught sight of Caitlin. "How's our patient doing?"

Caitlin blushed and dropped her eyes, but she answered in a normal voice. "Fine. Well, I'm worried about this spot here. The rest of the sores are healing, but this one's pretty red." She pointed to a scabby place on Abby's quivering hind leg.

Dr. Campbell examined the scab gently. "I see what you mean. I thought we had everything clean last time, but there must be something in there. A foxtail, maybe. I'm going to have to lance it."

"Well, okay. If you have to," Caitlin said, stroking the dog. "I'll hold her head to make sure she doesn't bite you."

"Doesn't bite *him*!" Jenna exclaimed. "What about you?"

Dr. Campbell laughed. "I'll be all right. Why don't you girls go sit in the waiting room?"

Jenna had already started for the door when she noticed out of the corner of her eye that Caitlin wasn't moving.

"I want to stay," Caitlin said in a low, determined voice.

"It's better if you don't," said the vet. "You might get sick. You might even faint—I've seen it happen before."

"I won't," Caitlin insisted. "I want to stay."

"I know, but that's what I have an assistant for," Dr. Campbell said gently. He opened the door and called, "Rhonda! Can you come in here, please?"

"Come on, Cat," Jenna urged. "Let's go wait like the doctor said."

Caitlin didn't budge. "I'm a big girl, Dr. Campbell, and Abby is my responsibility. I want to stay."

Jenna felt her jaw drop open. Was Caitlin talking back?

The vet looked her over a moment, then shrugged. "Suit yourself," he said. "But don't say I didn't warn you."

Rhonda came bustling into the room. "You needed me?" She looked only a little older than Caitlin, and her shiny black hair was pulled off her face with a neon yellow scrunchie.

The vet was already drawing a hypodermic needle full of fluid. "We're going to do a little exploration here," he said. "Hold the head while I inject this anesthetic. Hopefully Abby will let us do this without making us put her under."

Rhonda moved wordlessly to cradle Abby's head in a way that kept her from turning around, and Dr. Campbell sank the needle into a flap of skin in the dog's hind leg. Abby whimpered, and Jenna averted her eyes, but Caitlin didn't even flinch. She held her ground on the other side of the examination table, soothing Abby and steadying her hind leg.

The vet waited for the area to become numb, then removed a small scalpel from a drawer of instruments. Jenna took an involuntary step backward, away from the table, as he brought the shiny steel down on Abby's flesh. The dog made no cry— the Novocain was working—but Jenna felt a little queasy all the same. Backing slowly to the corner of the room, she sank into a chair to wait where she wouldn't have to see any blood.

She could still see everyone's faces, though. Dr. Campbell had put the scalpel down and was prodding with gloved fingers the area he'd just opened. Caitlin watched intently, her expression completely absorbed. Rhonda wasn't looking.

"Yep, that's what I thought," the vet muttered. "I think I see a foxtail." He picked up some long forceps and began digging around in the wound.

Jenna sniffed the air. A horrible smell had invaded the room.

"Yep, foxtail," he repeated. "Got it." He extracted the tweezers and held them up to reveal an impossibly long, goopy piece of what looked like straw. Jenna felt her stomach rise into her throat. She looked hurriedly away, toward Rhonda at Abby's head.

To Jenna's surprise, Rhonda looked almost as nauseated as Jenna felt. Not only was the assistant still not watching the vet, but her eyes were now fixed firmly, almost desperately, on the doorknob, and her tan cheeks had turned the color of ashes.

*It's that smell,* Jenna thought, trying to close her nose against the stink of infection that overwhelmed the small space. *How can Caitlin stand to be that close?*

But Caitlin not only seemed unaffected by the stench, she didn't even seem to notice. "So what are you going to do next?" she asked the vet quietly. "Does she need stitches?"

"No. We'll let that drain." He set aside his tools and began applying a dressing. "All done," he announced a minute later. "Thanks, Rhonda. You can go."

Rhonda nodded. Waiting only long enough for Caitlin to take Abby's head, she left the room without a word.

"And you thought Caitlin would faint!" Jenna couldn't resist reminding Dr. Campbell. "Your assistant was the one dying to get out of here. Caitlin's steady as a rock."

Dr. Campbell glanced briefly at Jenna, who was still holding down the chair in the corner, then turned his head to give Caitlin a long, curious look.

Caitlin withered noticeably under the doctor's scrutiny. She returned his gaze only an instant before staring down at the floor with a shy, self-conscious smile.

"Do you like all types of animals?" he asked.

Caitlin's head jerked back up. "Oh, yes. All types," she said passionately, forgetting her shyness again. "I love to help animals more than anything."

Dr. Campbell nodded. "How would you like a job?"

Ben glanced nervously at the clock, then ran a sweaty, impatient hand through his hair and returned his attention to his computer. It was getting really late. If his mom found out he was still awake, she'd never let him finish tonight. And he was so close now. So close. If he could just get this one stupid part to work. . . .

"Man, I wish Dad had finished this program," he muttered under his breath. "This wouldn't even be a challenge for him."

Luckily his father had taught him a ton about writing code, or Ben wouldn't have had a prayer. Of course, it also helped that the computer game he was attempting to finish was already 99.5 percent done.

It had come to Ben in a flash as he was changing for gym that afternoon. If he had to have a computer nerd for a father, why not take advantage of it? The programs his father developed at ComAm were all highly technical—some were even classified—and of no interest to the average human being. But computers weren't just Mr. Pipkin's job, they were also his hobby. And for the past year or so he'd been relaxing in the evenings by designing one of the coolest computer games Ben had ever seen.

He called the game A-Mazed, and it featured unbelievably detailed three-dimensional graphics. Players were whisked back to ancient Egypt, where they learned that, as expendable slaves, they'd been sealed in the tomb with a pharaoh. To save their own lives, they first had to find tools and light, escape the sealed chamber, and then work through the snakiest, most confused mess of tunnels ever designed. And that wasn't all—there was danger at every turn. An intricate network of booby traps designed to thwart would-be grave robbers stood ready to do double duty on any escaped slaves wandering through the pyramid.

The trick of the game was that a person had to go down before he could get out—down a hundred feet below the desert floor, where any false move could trigger a sandy cave-in and whole passages sometimes flooded with groundwater. It was against every human instinct to go down, into the earth, when common sense cried that the exit had to be up, toward the sun, but that was what made the game a challenge. That and the fact that there was a potentially fatal situation to deal with about every fifteen feet, no matter which way a player went. Mr. Pipkin had just finished the program the week before.

"Hey, Dad," Ben had asked at dinner. "Would it be all right if I gave copies of A-Mazed to a few of my friends? They could be beta testers for you, let you know what they think of it." Ben had been sure his father would say yes, but Mr. Pipkin had shaken his head.

"It's not ready yet, Ben. I'd love for your friends to play with it later, but I still have work to do before we unleash it on the public."

"Like what?" Ben had protested. "I thought it was all done!"

"There's some sort of bug in the code for the second flooding sequence, and I'm not sure the mummy on the fourth level is working right either," his father had replied with the engrossed, faraway look a computer glitch always inspired. "I'll have to work out the kinks and do a lot more testing before you give the program to anyone."

Ben's mother had frowned from across the table. "Why would you want to let a bunch of kids get their hands on it before it's copyrighted? I thought you were going to sell that one."

Mrs. Pipkin was the financial brains in the family. Without her constant reminders, Ben's father would have forgotten to bring home his paycheck half the time.

"I'll sell it when it's finished," Mr. Pipkin had agreed jovially, helping himself to more green beans. "But you have to have beta testers, Maude. It's all part of the process."

"So I *can* pass out a few copies, then?" Ben had broken in eagerly.

"Sure. In a month or two, after I've had a chance to fix the bugs."

"A month!" Ben had cried. He couldn't wait a month—he needed to be cool now! "But it's only those two little things, and—"

"It's your father's program, Benny." His mother had cut him off. "If you want my opinion, you're lucky he's sharing at all."

Sulking in his room after dinner, Ben hadn't felt even slightly lucky. He'd been counting on that program to do what his leather outfit, now safely hidden from his mother, hadn't accomplished: change his image. Obviously no one was ever going to believe he was tough, but if he could convince them he was *smart*—in the coolest, most avant-garde kind of way, of course—that might even be better. Smart he could probably live up to.

And that was when he'd decided to finish his father's program himself. If he couldn't flood a few corridors and make a mummy run around, then his name wasn't Ben Pipkin! Sneaking a copy of the most recent version from his father's study, Ben had brought the game back up to his room, loaded it on his own computer, and set to work.

He'd been at it for hours now. The flooding sequence had proved fairly easy to fix, but the stupid mummy was driving him crazy. He wasn't even exactly sure what was wrong—it just seemed to show up in unexpected places and stand still when it ought to chase the slaves.

"Come on," he muttered impatiently, glancing at the clock again. It was after midnight! If his parents woke up, he was dead.

And then he had a brilliant idea: Why not delete the mummy altogether? It wasn't really needed, not with all the other stuff going on. He returned to the file that controlled the mummy and made some quick revisions.

"There!" he breathed at last. Relaunching the game, he hurriedly navigated to the fourth level. No mummy. "Yes!" he exclaimed in a whisper. "I did it!"

There were just a couple of things left. Returning to the code, he deleted the name A-Mazed from the title sequence. *Too wimpy—I told Dad it needed something cooler.* He thought a moment. *I know! Tomb of Terror!* Ben's tired eyes shone as he typed the new name on his keyboard. *Oh, yeah. That's a lot better.*

He opened the high score file next and quickly added some code to keep his name at the top. Then, his hands shaking with excitement, he logged on to the CCHS Web site and opened the guest book. A short time later the game had been downloaded, there for the taking by anyone who wanted it.

TOMB OF TERROR! THE HOTTEST NEW COMPUTER GAME IN THE NATION, AND YOU GET IT FIRST, YOU GET IT FREE, Ben wrote in the caption. AS VIRTUAL AS REALITY GETS, WITH STATE-OF-THE-ART 3D PROGRAMMING BY BENJAMIN PIPKIN. He smiled at that last part—for once being Ben junior would come in handy. Could he help it if people assumed *he* was the programmer? But just to make sure they did, he snapped a quick, glasses-free picture of himself with his father's digital camera, doctored the image to make himself look better, then posted it next to his notice for the game.

It was done.

*I'm a genius*, he congratulated himself as he climbed, exhausted, into bed. *That game's going to spread like wildfire, and so is my new, cool reputation.*

A moment later he was sound asleep, a dreamy smile on his face.

# Five

Jenna heard footsteps flying up the stairs to her third-floor bedroom on Thursday morning. It was the only warning she got before Caitlin burst through her door without knocking.

"What do you think?" Caitlin asked breathlessly, whirling around so that Jenna could view her from all angles. "Do I look like a veterinarian's assistant?"

Jenna smiled despite the invasion of her privacy. Caitlin was so thrilled about her first day of work with Dr. Campbell that it was impossible to be anything but happy for her.

"I think you look real nice," Jenna said, taking in Caitlin's immaculately combed light brown hair and the bright yellow uniform smock Dr. Campbell had provided. "Are you sure you want to wear white pants, though?" she added dubiously. "I mean, they look fine, and they're real medical and everything, but I thought you were going to be cleaning out kennels."

Caitlin glanced down at her spotless white slacks.

"You're right. I'll go change." She was off, pounding back down the two flights of stairs before Jenna could say another thing. Jenna checked her Spirit Week outfit of a gold turtleneck and overdyed green jeans in the mirror one last time, then went downstairs too.

When Jenna walked into the kitchen, everyone but Caitlin was already gathered there, eager for the pancake breakfast Mrs. Conrad had promised in honor of Caitlin's new job. Maggie and Allison were pacing around poking their noses into everything, Mr. Conrad was reading the newspaper at the counter, and Sarah was practicing pirouettes in her new slick-footed pajamas.

"Can I help?" Jenna asked, wandering through the crowd and idly opening the refrigerator door.

"You can get out of my way. That would help," Mrs. Conrad replied, pointing her spatula toward the dining room, where the table was already set. "And take the orange juice and your sisters with you."

"Why?" Allison whined. "We're not doing anything!"

"Precisely," Mr. Conrad said, peering over the top of his paper.

Maggie tossed her long curls indignantly as she walked past him into the dining room.

Jenna had just finished pouring seven glasses of orange juice when Caitlin bounded into the dining room in a pair of sharply creased brown pants. "How are these?" she demanded.

"You look very nice," Mrs. Conrad answered, walking into the room with a heaping platter of pancakes. "And your timing is perfect."

"I don't know about that," their father teased, bringing up the rear with the bacon and scrambled eggs. "If you'd been a little later, that would have meant more for us."

Caitlin giggled happily and took her usual place at the table.

"No, the place of honor!" her mother insisted, setting the platter down. "After all, this is your big day."

Caitlin blushed but moved to her father's seat at the head of the table. Mr. Conrad took Caitlin's chair. Then everyone else sat down and began dishing out the breakfast Mrs. Conrad had prepared.

"Who'll say grace?" Mr. Conrad asked. "Caitlin, how about you?"

Caitlin bowed her head eagerly. "Father, we thank you for this food, for each other, and for the many special blessings you bring us every day. Amen."

"Amen," her family repeated. They sat surveying the meal in front of them a moment longer, savoring the festive occasion; then everyone dug in.

"So when do you get to operate on the animals?" Sarah asked Caitlin, her mouth full of pancake.

71

"Never!" Caitlin's light brown eyes were round at the mere idea. "My main job is to care for the animals that are boarding or staying for treatment—and to clean out the kennels and examination rooms."

Maggie made a face.

"But I'll also get to hold the animals or pass tools to Dr. Campbell when he's doing certain procedures," Caitlin hurried to add. "I'll get to see everything he does."

"It's going to be perfect," Jenna couldn't resist putting in, since she'd been there to hear the entire job offer. "His other assistant, Rhonda, prefers paperwork, and since the practice is growing, she's going to take over all the reception and billing and leave the animals to Caitlin."

"That's the best part," Caitlin admitted shyly. "I won't have to talk to anyone except Rhonda and Dr. Campbell. Oh, and I can keep Ab—uh, the dog—in the back room during the day while I'm working too."

"You *still* have to find that animal another home," Mrs. Conrad said.

"I know," Caitlin agreed. "But in the meantime . . ." She paused and drew in a deep breath, a radiant smile on her face. "The whole thing is so perfect, it seems almost heaven-sent."

Their father looked up with a half smile. "Don't rule that out," he advised.

The idea hit Jenna with unexpected force. After all, hadn't Caitlin prayed and prayed about finding a job? And how else could a person explain the entire weird chain of coincidences that had led Caitlin to this moment? When that scrawny mutt first walked into the warehouse, who could have foreseen that timid Caitlin would defy Jesse to be its rescuer, or that she would brave her mother's certain anger by bringing the sad thing home? But by some miracle—*was* it a miracle?—Mrs. Conrad had let it stay, and Caitlin had gone even further out of character by taking the stray to a vet by herself. And of all the vets in the phone book, the one Caitlin had happened to pick—at random?—just happened to be one with a growing practice and a weak-stomached assistant, one who just happened to notice as he was removing a random foxtail from a random dog that Caitlin might make a pretty good addition to his staff.

*Well, actually*, Jenna thought, *he didn't notice that part as much as I pointed it out. Who knows what would have happened if I hadn't decided to tag along? For that matter, Caitlin wouldn't have been at the warehouse to rescue that dog in the first place if it hadn't been for me.*

But a moment later Jenna realized that her interference didn't make things less mysterious at all. Hadn't she prayed to be able to help Caitlin somehow?

*And I did,* she thought, an amazed smile on her face.

Nicole sniffed back the last of her tears and wiped her streaming makeup with an already sodden wad of toilet paper.

*When am I going to learn?* she berated herself. Dropping the wet paper into the toilet, she grabbed a fresh length of tissue from the roll in the girls' room stall and dabbed away the last damp traces of melted mascara.

She should have known better than to try to talk to Jesse during the lunchtime spirit rally, but she'd been desperate. He hadn't so much as looked at her since he'd dropped her off after the Eight Prime meeting on Tuesday, and here it was, already Thursday.

*He still hasn't looked at me,* Nicole thought bitterly, in danger of crying all over again. All she had wanted was to say hello, to make sure things weren't going to be weird between them now. But Jesse had been hanging out with Gary Baldwin and a couple of other Wildcats and hadn't wanted to be bothered.

The football players had made a tight little knot of green jerseys as they watched the cheerleaders run through a series of yells. Melanie was cheering with the squad again, looking even prettier than before her injury, and it had been clear who everyone's eyes were on. Nicole knew Jesse was trying to reestablish his friendships on the team, and she'd been pretty sure she ought to leave him alone. But the combination of her already rampant insecurity with Jesse's obvious interest in Melanie was ultimately more than she could stand. She had crashed his group anyway.

*A lot of good it did me, too.* She pulled still more toilet paper from the roll and blew her nose. Sure, Jesse had said hi, but without taking his eyes off the cheerleaders, and after that all she'd managed to get out of him was the odd, distracted *hmmm*. She had finally run off, humiliated, to spend the rest of lunchtime crying in the bathroom. The most depressing part was, she was pretty sure he hadn't even noticed.

She gave her nose one last blast, flushed all the tissues, and opened the stall door. She was still washing up at one of the chipped sinks when the door burst open and Jenna Conrad rushed in, her normally creamy cheeks flushed red.

"Jenna, what's the matter?" Nicole asked.

Jenna pulled up short, clearly surprised to see her. "Ni-Nicole," she stammered. "Why aren't you at the rally?"

Nicole shrugged and turned off the water. "Why aren't you?" she countered.

Jenna glanced around the empty bathroom as if to make sure they were alone. "I guess I just wasn't in the mood."

She already seemed calmer than when she'd first come in, but Nicole was certain something was wrong. A blush still stained Jenna's full cheeks, and she'd made no move at all to use the facilities.

"Yeah. I wasn't in the mood either," said Nicole. "How many times can a person watch every guy in school drool over Melanie Andrews?"

She hadn't known she was going to say it, and the moment the words were out of her mouth, she regretted the catty remark. Would Jenna be offended? Would she tell Melanie?

But to Nicole's amazement, Jenna only nodded. "I know what you mean," she said.

"You do?" Nicole blurted out.

A small, sheepish smile crept onto Jenna's features. "What have *you* got against her?"

*Where to start?* Nicole wondered. And how much should she tell Jenna? "I just . . . well, I wouldn't mind maybe going out with Jesse sometime. If it worked out, I mean. But all he thinks about is Melanie." She hesitated a moment, wondering if she ought to admit she'd asked him to the homecoming dance. No. If she did, she'd also have to confess that he'd told her they were just friends, and that was too demeaning to repeat.

"I have noticed Jesse seems pretty interested in Melanie. But I didn't know you liked him, Nicole."

"I wouldn't say I *liked* him," Nicole hedged, wary of putting too much trust in Jenna's ability to keep a secret. "It's just . . . I wouldn't mind, that's all. But I'll bet you anything he's only hanging around out there right now to try to find out if Melanie's picked her date for the homecoming dance."

To Nicole's surprise, her comment brought the color rushing back to Jenna's cheeks. "Oh, she's picked a date, all right," Jenna said, in a strange, constricted voice. "She's going with Peter."

"*Your* Peter?"

Jenna looked away. "Peter and I are just friends."

"Still!" Nicole exclaimed. "I can't believe he asked her!" *And I really can't believe she said yes!* she added silently.

"He didn't. She asked him," Jenna murmured, her eyes on the floor.

Nicole was all but speechless. "That . . . that's so weird," she said at last. "So who are you going with, then?"

Jenna shook her head, her eyes still not meeting Nicole's. "I'm not going. Peter and I usually go to dances together. And it's not a big deal or anything, but . . . I don't really feel like going anymore."

"I know exactly what you mean," Nicole admitted

in a low voice. Jenna's obvious honesty made her feel like confiding more too. "Can you keep something to yourself, without telling Peter or *anyone*?"

Jenna looked up and nodded.

"I asked Jesse to the dance, but he turned me down."

"He did?" Jenna's blue eyes were full of sympathy.

"Well, that's how it goes." Nicole tried to shrug it off, but she could feel tears beginning to clog her throat again. "Hey, I have an idea. Since neither of us is going to the dance, why don't you come over Saturday night? We can rent some videos or something."

"I don't know. . . ."

"Come on," Nicole urged. "I don't want to be alone. Do you?"

For the first time since she'd stormed in, Jenna smiled. "Not really. Okay, why not? We'll have fun."

"Right!"

"Besides, there's no way I can stay home that night. Maggie will be sure it's some kind of divine justice because I made her miss the Fall Fantasy."

"Can you believe they're still doing that hokey thing?" Nicole scoffed.

"Just do me a favor—don't ever even mention it in front of Maggie. And if you tell her you think it's hokey . . . well, you're seriously on your own."

They exchanged a few horror stories about the difficulties of living with younger sisters, and after Jenna left, and Nicole was alone again in the deserted bathroom, she was glad she'd invited her new friend to keep her company Saturday night. Courtney was going to the dance with Jeff—of course—and even if she hadn't been, there was no way Nicole could ever have told her that she'd actually asked Jesse out and had been turned down.

Jenna was a much more sympathetic listener.

"So, Leah, I can't believe Miguel has been keeping you a secret all this time," Mrs. del Rios teased, glancing playfully at her son across the dessert dishes. "I hope we'll be seeing a lot more of you from now on."

Leah heard the implied invitation in her voice with a surge of happiness and relief. "Thank you. I hope so too," she said sincerely.

As much as she'd been looking forward to going to the del Rios home, she'd been more than a little nervous when the big night had finally arrived. The hardest part had been pretending to listen carefully to the directions Miguel had given her to his house and showing the right amount of surprise when he'd finally revealed that he lived in the housing authority project. She had to make it look as though she had never suspected—the last thing she wanted now was for him to know she'd spied on him—while at the same time making it clear that where he lived didn't matter in the slightest.

"It's not like we're going to be hanging out around here all the time or anything," Miguel told his mother now. "So don't get any ideas."

Rosa rolled her eyes. "You already promised Mom you'd let her take your picture before the dance on Saturday, Miguel," she reminded him. "So I guess Leah will be here again in two days."

"That's right," said Mrs. del Rios. "And I'm going to hold you to it."

"Don't worry," Leah said with a grin. "I'll be here. In fact, my father said I could use his car again that night, so why don't I come over here first, and then we can drive it to the dance?"

"That's okay. I can drive," Miguel said, not catching the hint.

But Rosa did. "Or not!" she exclaimed. "Why would you take our old piece of junk when Leah's dad's car is so nice?" Mr. Rosenthal's brown Ford was parked under the streetlight in front of the house, visible through the living room window. "You can't expect a U.S. Girl to ride to a fancy dance in a clunker."

Leah stifled her groan behind a smile. Despite her protests, Miguel had insisted on telling his family about the modeling contest she'd won a couple of weeks before. She still wasn't comfortable with the idea of being the Missouri representative of the U.S. Girls clothing chain, and every time she thought about the January finals in California, her stomach turned over. Her, a model? Ridiculous! She'd have dropped out long before if not for the scholarships the final five winners would get. It was easy to walk away from fame and facials and too much makeup. It was much harder to give up on fifteen thousand dollars a year.

"I guess you're right," Miguel muttered to his sister. "All right, Leah. We'll take your dad's car."

Then Mrs. del Rios stood up, and everyone else rose to help carry the dirty dishes to the sink. Miguel's mother insisted on washing them herself, though, in spite of his protests that he'd do them after Leah left.

"I can help," Leah offered. "Why don't you and I do them together?"

But Mrs. del Rios shooed them both out of the kitchen. They ended up in the living room, where they were joined by Rosa.

"Why don't you go help Mom?" Miguel asked his sister. "Better yet, why don't you go do the dishes for her?"

"Because she said she wanted to do them herself," Rosa replied. "I guess she can do what she wants."

Miguel gave his sister a sharp look.

"She's not an invalid, Miguel! Besides, if she wanted me to do it, I'd do it."

"I need to leave in a minute anyway," Leah said uneasily, not sure why the dishes were such a big deal.

"There's no hurry," Rosa assured her. "Miguel just likes to worry. He's been this way ever since we found out Mom needs a transplant, and that's been two whole years. You'd think he'd have worn himself out by now."

"A transplant?" Leah repeated, stunned.

Rosa took in Leah's amazed expression with equal surprise on her own part. "Yeah, a kidney transplant. Mom's on dialysis three times a week."

She turned accusingly to her brother. "What's up with you, Miguel? Don't you tell anybody anything?"

# Six

"Hey, Pipkin. Pipkin, over here!"

Ben froze in the Friday cafeteria line, his hand involuntarily squeezing a carton of milk. He wasn't sure anyone had ever yelled his name in the cafeteria before. He wasn't sure it was such a good idea, either.

Slowly, his pulse pounding, Ben turned in the direction of the voice. Three reasonably cool-looking guys were eating together at the end of a nearby table, and one of them was waving for him to come join them.

"Me?" Ben mouthed, glancing back over his shoulder to see if they meant someone else. There was only a cafeteria lady in a hair net, who held out an impatient hand for his milk money. He paid her. Then, milk clutched in one hand and sack lunch in the other, he walked cautiously in the direction of the guy who had called him.

"Hey," a tall, lanky upperclassman greeted him as he shuffled to their table. "You're the Tomb of Terror guy, right? That game is awesome! I down-loaded it yesterday and ended up getting no home-work done at all."

"Really?"

Ben stopped suspecting an attack, but his heart, which a moment before had pounded with fear, still beat just as fast—with excitement. These guys didn't want to abuse him, they wanted to compliment him!

"Yeah. Shove over, Stuart. Let Benjamin sit down."

The guy sitting nearest Ben scooted over a little, leaving a place on the end of the bench. Ben took the still-warm spot in a daze. His plan was working!

"My name's Neil, by the way, and this is Lance," the first guy said. He was sitting across the table from Ben, and he pointed to the boy next to him.

Lance nodded and Ben nodded back, doing his best to look calm. "You don't have to call me Benjamin. Ben is fine."

"So, how did you come up with that game, any-way?" Stuart asked. "I thought I knew a lot about computers, but *man*—you leave me in the dust."

"Oh . . . there's really nothing to it, once you learn a little basic code," Ben bluffed, hoping they weren't going to question him too closely. His throat was unnaturally dry, and he risked opening his milk to take a sip before he went on. "I'm glad you like it, though. Did you figure out how to get out of the pyramid?"

"Are you kidding?" Neil asked. "It took me until midnight just to get out of the burial chamber!"

"I logged on last night to see if anyone knew how to light the torch," Lance reported, "and there were all kinds of people playing it."

"Really?" Ben said delightedly.

"Yeah. You ought to check for messages in the guest book when you get home," Neil suggested. "I'll bet you have a ton of—"

"What I don't understand," Stuart broke in, impatient with their small talk, "is how to get from the first to the second level. The passage goes straight up, and it's too slippery to climb."

Ben knew exactly the spot Stuart meant. He'd knocked himself out trying to solve the same problem when his dad had first designed that part. Of course, the irony was that going up at all was a waste of time, but there *was* a way to do it. There was a way to do everything, if a person was sufficiently determined.

"You can't climb it," Ben confirmed. "But you *can* get up it. What you need to do is—"

"No!" Neil butted in. "No, don't tell us! Geez, Stuart, you've only been trying one day and you're already whining for clues? Take all the fun out of it, why don't you?"

"Sliding backward down a slimy rock for two hours hardly classifies as fun," Stuart grumbled, but Ben could tell by his tone that the guy would be back at it the second he got home. He was hooked. By the looks on their faces, they all were.

"I like the part where you have to roll under that big stone door right before it closes," Lance volunteered.

"Oh, yeah. That part is really cool!" Ben agreed, temporarily forgetting that, as the game's designer, he ought to be more modest. "I mean, uh, programming it was a challenge," he added awkwardly.

Neil shook his head disbelievingly. "Are you kidding me? You must be a programming *genius*."

"Not really," Ben said with a dismissive wave of his hand.

Unfortunately, there wasn't room at the table for his gesture. The back of his hand smacked into the side of his open milk carton, sending it reeling toward Stuart. Ben watched, horrified, as Lance's hand shot out from across the table, catching the carton just before it overturned. But even Lance's spectacular save couldn't stop the splash of milk that escaped, drenching his wrist and drowning the Jell-O on Stuart's tray.

"Hey!" Stuart said, staring irritably from his Jell-O to Ben.

Ben could feel his cheeks turning crimson, the way they always did when he pulled one of his boneheaded stunts. "I'm sorry," he murmured. For the first time, he missed the way his thick glasses had hidden his eyes from view. "It was an accident."

The other guys were silent. The mood at the table had become decidedly tense. In one careless instant, Ben had transformed himself from an interesting guy who designed computer games back into a clumsy nerd who spilled his milk. He needed to say something, *anything,* to convince them he was cool again.

"Uh, sorry about your Jell-O, Stuart. But the good thing is, you know, gelatin is relatively impermeable."

"Relatively im-*what?*" Stuart repeated, not looking any happier about the situation.

"Impermeable. It's, uh . . . well . . . never mind."

Ben snuck glances at Neil and Lance. They continued to regard him with altered expressions, as if not sure they wanted him to stay. Ben's cheeks burned even hotter. He was seriously considering excusing himself and running for the sanctuary of the soccer field when a vision in green and gold stopped at the end of their table—Angela Maldonado in her cheerleading outfit.

"Hi, Ben," she said with a friendly smile. "I saw your game on the school Web site. How cool!"

"Uh, well, thanks," he said, his heart beating double time. Ben thought Angela was the most beautiful of the cheerleaders, not to mention the nicest. If he had been a different kind of guy—a *vastly* different kind of guy—he might have tried for her. The way things stood, though, it was a miracle he even knew her to say hello.

"You'll have to tell me how you did it sometime," she said before she continued on her way.

His eyes followed her a few yards before returning timidly to his lunch companions. But once again, their expressions had changed completely.

"You know Angela Maldonado?" Lance said. "Sweet!"

Neil and Stuart nodded emphatic agreement.

"Angela is, uh, just a friend," Ben told them, blushing anew. "I only met her because she's on the cheerleading squad with another friend of mine, Melanie Andrews."

"You're friends with Melanie *Andrews*?" Stuart said, his ruined Jell-O completely forgotten. "Hey, so are you going to eat with us or what?"

He pointed to Ben's still unopened lunch bag. "Take out your sandwich and stay awhile."

"Finally!" Vanessa complained in the locker room before the big game on Friday. "I thought she'd *never* get out of here!"

"She's not that bad," Lou Anne Simmons said, touching up her makeup.

Vanessa shot her a look worth a thousand words.

"If you like that bossy, hyperefficient type, I mean," Lou Anne amended uneasily.

88

Melanie shook her head. All week long their new coach had been working overtime to get the squad in top form for the homecoming game. And now that the game was within minutes of starting, all Vanessa could do was put her down.

"That girl wouldn't know gratitude if it bit her in the butt," Melanie whispered to Tanya Jeffries.

Tanya giggled. "Vanessa acts like something's perpetually biting her in the butt," she whispered back. "And I'm pretty sure it isn't gratitude."

"I can't believe Sandra changed our halftime dance around," Vanessa griped, unaware of their conversation. "The choreography is hopeless now." Vanessa, of course, had been the original choreographer.

"I think it's better," Melanie said, fed up.

Her words provoked a sudden silence. The other girls stopped getting ready for the game and looked nervously toward Vanessa.

But Vanessa didn't rise to the insult. Instead, she changed the subject.

"Oh, I forgot to tell you guys. I'm not going to the dance with Ricky Black anymore," she said. Her eyes held Melanie's strangely, as if the news in some way answered Melanie's critique. "I'm going with Jesse Jones now."

The group erupted in confused exclamations.

"Jesse!" Angela cried with a furtive glance at Melanie. "But Ricky asked you last week!"

"Jesse!" Melanie protested. "You said he was a total flirt!"

Vanessa shrugged, her eyes never leaving Melanie's. "Things change," she said, loading the words with undue importance.

Melanie couldn't believe her ears. Jesse and *Vanessa*? Wasn't Vanessa the one who had warned her that Jesse was a guy to steer clear of? And now she was breaking off a preexisting date to go out with him herself?

Melanie shuddered, feeling a little twinge of . . . something. Then she shook her head.

*If ever two people deserved each other*, she thought, *it has to be those two*.

"You don't mind, do you, Melanie?" Vanessa asked, false sugar in her voice. "I mean, you did say you wouldn't date Jesse Jones if he were the last man left on earth."

"And I meant every word," Melanie said quickly. "You go right ahead, Vanessa—have a great time. In fact, you know what? I think you and Jesse will make a perfect couple."

"Jenna! It's Peter!" Allison shouted from downstairs Friday evening.

"Peter? Here?"

Jenna sat up on her bed, scattering homework assignments in her haste. The essay she'd been writing for English class slid forgotten off her lap, and her geometry book hit the floor with a thud. All week long, ever since she'd found out Peter was taking Melanie to the dance, Jenna had been avoiding him. One day it had been a quiz she'd needed to study for; another, extra practice in choir—anything she could think of to get out of those lunchtime rallies in the quad, rallies for the Friday game that only reminded her of the Saturday dance. She had no idea why Peter was showing up at her house now, unannounced, but she still didn't feel like talking to him.

With a sigh, she got up and went downstairs.

Allison had left Peter standing alone inside the entryway. When Jenna walked in, he started to smile—then he got a better look at her.

"You aren't ready," he said, taking in the rumpled sweatpants and stretched-out thermal top she'd changed into after dinner.

"Ready for what?" Jenna asked irritably.

"You're kidding, right?" he replied incredulously. "How could you forget the homecoming game and bonfire?"

"I didn't forget. I just wasn't planning to go."

"You weren't?" The look on Peter's face changed gradually from disbelief to annoyance. "You might have let me know, then. We always go to the games together."

"Sure. Like we always go to the dances together, right?"

91

"Is that what you're playing at now?" Peter was angry, which was unusual, and letting it show, which was rarer still. "I'm sorry, Jenna, but the way the rules keep changing, I don't know what I'm supposed to do with you and what I'm not."

"The rules aren't changing," Jenna protested. "We always go to dances togeth—"

"So if Miguel del Rios had asked you, you'd have turned him down and gone with me instead?"

"Peter!" she shushed him, her heart skipping for fear that one of her nosy sisters might be eavesdropping. "You promised to keep that to yourself!"

"I don't see anyone but us," Peter said, gesturing around the empty foyer.

"I'm not going to talk about it here," she said stubbornly.

"Then come out and talk in the car," he said. "For crying out loud, Jenna, you can't avoid me forever."

"Who's avoiding who? *I'm* not the one making plans with other people."

Peter raised his eyebrows and nodded toward the door.

Jenna glowered a moment, then shrugged. "Fine," she said, walking past him to yank it open.

Outside, the autumn night was crisp and cold. Jenna hugged her loose shirt around her and ran to Peter's Toyota. Letting herself into its still-warm interior, she slammed the passenger door while Peter climbed in from the other side.

"So. I still don't understand why we aren't going to the game," he said, glancing at his watch. "It's *homecoming*, Jenna. And we're missing it."

"If you want to go, go. No one's stopping you."

Peter made an aggravated face. "I'm trying to be a friend, but you're not making it easy."

Jenna only folded her arms across her chest and stared straight ahead through the slowly fogging windshield.

"Look, I'm sorry now that I told Melanie I'd go to the dance with her. If I'd had any idea how upset you were going to be, I never would have done it. But I can't back out when she's counting on me. And I don't think you're being very fair."

Jenna's expression didn't change, but in her heart she knew Peter was right. He couldn't go back on his word, and she *wasn't* being very fair. It just made her feel bad that he would put Melanie's feelings ahead of hers.

"And you know you'd have gone with Miguel," Peter added. "I didn't hear you denying that."

"That's different!" Jenna cried. "That's different because I liked Miguel, and . . ."

But the sentence hung between them, unfinished. Was it different? Or did Peter feel the same way about Melanie? Jenna wasn't laughing at that possibility anymore. On the contrary, it scared her to death. She didn't want to lose her best friend—not now, not when she needed him so much.

"Jenna, I honestly don't know if it's different or not." Peter sounded worn out. "I only know that I don't want to fight with you anymore. I mean, we're still friends, right?"

"Of course."

"So can't we please just go to the game and have a good time? I don't want to miss that, or the bonfire, either, and it won't be any fun without you."

"Really?"

"Really." He smiled, and it was almost his old familiar smile. "So you have exactly five seconds to go change your clothes, or I'm taking you looking like that." He put his hand on the ignition, as if about to turn the key. "One . . . two . . ."

"I'm going, I'm going!" Jenna cried, jumping out of the car and running through the chilly night to her front door.

*I'm going!* she thought happily, pounding up the stairs to her bedroom.

But as she pulled on a sweater and jeans and forced a brush through her brown hair, all her doubts came rushing back.

Were things back to normal with Peter?

Or next year would they both be at the game with different people?

"You're going to the concession stand *now*?" Courtney Bell said. "The game's almost over." She gestured down toward the field, as if to prove her point, then smoothed her red hair, which was frizzing wildly in the cold. The night air had put patches of pink on Courtney's pale cheeks, and her eyes seemed brighter in contrast, nearly matching the apple green angora that peeked through her open coat.

"So then I'll beat the crowd, won't I?" Nicole replied, beginning to edge sideways through the packed bleachers.

"Get me some gum," Courtney called to her over the crowd noise. "And a Coke for Jeff!" She pointed to her boyfriend at her side.

"Yeah, yeah," Nicole muttered under her breath. She knew she should be grateful to Courtney for letting her tag along on her big homecoming date, but gratitude was the last thing she felt just then. Disgust was closer to the mark—disgust at Jesse, at life . . . but mostly at herself.

*I'm not even hungry*, she thought as she wandered toward the concession stand, all but oblivious to the game being played on the field below. The Wildcats were winning—that was the only part that had made an impression. That and the cold, which stiffened her knuckles inside her green-and-gold knit gloves and made fantastical billows of the players' heated breath.

*I don't even want anything.* But she knew she would eat anyway. She'd gobble down some candy or some fat-drenched snack from the fryer, the same way she'd eaten the pizza she didn't want before the game, the ice cream and soda she didn't want at halftime, and handfuls of caramel corn from Courtney's huge bag every time it was passed her way.

"I don't even like caramel corn," Nicole groaned, a hand on her bloated stomach. She could feel her flesh pressing forward, and she was glad for the parka that covered everything under a thick, shapeless layer of down. "I don't like it that much, anyway."

But even with a stomach so full she was feeling half sick—even with the dim understanding that she was only punishing herself for her failure with Jesse—she got in the concession stand line to eat again.

"I'll have some M&M's, a pack of gum, and a large Coke," Nicole told the guy who took her order. "Oh, and some Red Vines."

He rang it into the register. "That'll be four-fifty."

Nicole tried to shove a hand into her front pants pocket, but there wasn't room. She had to take off her glove and suck in her stomach to force her stiff fingers to the bottom, and then the denim pocket edge scraped up the back of her hand. Somehow she managed to extract a five-dollar bill and pay.

*I should have made Court come help me with this stuff,* she thought as she filled her jacket pockets with the candy. Then, her hands back in her gloves, Nicole picked up the Coke. *Not that she could tear herself away from Jeff.*

Ever since Courtney had met Jeff Nguyen, all she ever thought about was him. It was depressing simply to be around such a nauseatingly happy couple, and Nicole was in no hurry to return. Instead she walked over to the chain-link fence, where a small crowd stood watching the action on the nearby field. It wasn't a great vantage point. At that low elevation, she couldn't see much besides the bobbing gold helmets of the Wildcats and the midnight blue ones of the players from Sycamore Ridge.

"Are we still winning?" she asked a guy in a CCHS jacket.

"We've won," he told her. "There's only a minute left and we have a two-touchdown lead."

"A minute?"

She hadn't realized the game was *that* close to over. Alarmed, she hurried back toward the stands. She didn't want to lose track of Courtney and Jeff when everyone started pouring out of the bleachers to go to the postgame bonfire in the dirt at the edge of the student parking lot. A big area had been roped off to keep it free of cars, and everyone would be heading that way as soon as the game ended.

Nicole couldn't imagine anything more pathetic than showing up there completely on her own.

*Unless it's showing up as a third wheel on my best friend's date*, she reflected unhappily. Homecoming was hardly turning out to be the romantic occasion she'd envisioned.

The final buzzer sounded on the field, and the bleachers erupted in a frenzy of cheering, followed by a mad rush toward the bonfire site. Nicole barely managed to hook up with Courtney and Jeff amid the surging crowd.

"Here's your Coke," she told him, happy to get rid of it. She was already cold enough without carrying a cupful of ice around.

"Thanks." Jeff's jet black hair reflected the stadium lights as he bent to take the drink. "How much do I owe you?"

"Forget it."

"My gum?" Courtney queried, raising one plucked brow.

Nicole handed it over, then ripped into her M&M's.

"What happened to the diet?" Courtney teased as the crowd pushed them along toward the parking lot. "What is that? About a million and fourteen calories so far tonight?"

"Look who's talking," Nicole retorted. Even bloated, she was still thinner than Courtney.

Jeff laughed, and Courtney punched him in the arm.

At the bonfire, a huge pyre of grocery pallets sent incandescent sparks into the inky sky. Nicole shoved chocolate into her mouth while the familiar smell of wood smoke did strange things to her emotions. She pressed closer to the flames, but she still felt separated from the festivities somehow—almost as if she were watching them on TV.

The adults who had built the fire were rushing back and forth in their CCHS Boosters jackets, and her excited classmates blurred into a sea of green and gold. Soon the players would show up, freshly showered and full of boasts about their undefeated season. Coach Davis would make a victory speech about Wildcat spirit, and the cheerleaders would burn a paper effigy of a Lakeview football player to signify victory in the next week's game. Everyone was talking and laughing happily, thrilled with the Wildcats' big win. The positive energy in the crowd was almost palpable.

But Nicole just couldn't get into it.

She glanced sideways at Courtney and Jeff—at the happy couples all around her—and polished off the M&M's by pouring them into her mouth all at once. She tossed the empty wrapper into the fire and watched it burn before she pulled the licorice out of her pocket and started working on that.

Courtney leaned over to whisper in her ear. "I know what'll cheer you up. Jesse alert, dead ahead!"

"Jesse? Here?"

Nicole had been certain that Jesse would be a no-show at the bonfire—she couldn't imagine him showing up to hear any victory speeches after Coach Davis had kept him off the field for the game. But there he was on the other side of the fire, cool and handsome in his letterman's jacket. And there she was, bloated beyond recognition. With a quick, convulsive gesture, Nicole tossed her licorice into the flames.

"Hey!" Courtney protested. "You could have offered it to us!"

But Nicole ignored her. "What's he doing here?" she wondered aloud.

"Why don't you go find out?"

Nicole hung back, trying to decide. Jesse looked inviting standing off by himself in the flickering light of the fire . . . but how many times could a girl get burned?

She finally adjusted her parka over her bulging stomach and started walking toward him, but she was only halfway there when the cheerleaders arrived, flushed and triumphant from the game, whooping and hollering to attract all eyes. Nicole's steps faltered as the girls crowded toward the fireside, pushing and laughing. Melanie was near the front, near Jesse, and not until she'd given him a wide berth did Nicole start walking again.

She was only a few steps away when, out of the darkness behind him, two green-and-gold sweatered arms encircled Jesse's waist, two green-and-gold manicured hands clasped tightly over his abs, and Vanessa Winters's chin appeared over his shoulder. She snuggled her face into his neck. "Guess who?" she teased.

Nicole stared with mounting horror. Vanessa Winters? What was the cheerleading captain doing with her arms around Jesse? More importantly, why wasn't he moving away? Swallowing what little pride she had left, Nicole moved the last few feet around the edge of the fire until she was face-to-face with the unlikely couple.

"Hi, Jesse," she said, struggling to ignore the way Vanessa was clinging to him, as if she needed his support to keep standing. "I didn't expect to see you here tonight."

A flash of annoyance crossed Jesse's face, and Nicole realized too late that she shouldn't even have alluded to his suspension from the team. The fact that everyone already knew about it was obviously never going to sink in.

"He *had* to come," Vanessa said. Did that girl have more than two hands, or were they simply everywhere? "Since I'm going to the dance with

101

him, the least he could do was keep me company here at the bonfire."

"You guys are going to the dance together?" It sounded like someone else's voice: uninterested, emotionless—exactly the opposite of the way she felt.

Vanessa crinkled her nose and hugged Jesse even tighter. "That's right. Although he's lucky I'm so understanding. I had to break a perfectly good date to go with him."

Jesse gently extricated himself from Vanessa's grasp, putting an arm across her shoulders instead. "You know I wanted to ask you earlier, Vee," he said in a low voice. "I just didn't think you'd say yes. I've been working up my nerve for weeks."

Nicole's jaw dropped, but Jesse's expression warned her to keep quiet.

Vanessa giggled. "Isn't he adorable?"

"Yeah." *For a liar!* Nicole wanted to scream. *For a big, self-centered, I-can't-even-believe-what-I'm-hearing-liar! He hasn't wanted to take you for weeks—he wasn't even going until I talked him into it!*

She'd been totally blindsided. Jesse didn't like Melanie better than her—Jesse liked *anyone* better than her! And Vanessa wasn't even that great. Aside from being captain of the cheerleaders . . .

"I have to go," Nicole said abruptly.

She forced herself to walk slowly until she was out of the crowd, beyond the ring of firelight, and then she ran. Tears burned her eyelids and stung her cheeks. She swiped at them and kept going blindly. She had to get away. Away from Jesse, from Vanessa, from everything. . . .

A small lighted bathroom building loomed into view at the edge of the lot. Nicole headed toward it. Girls were smoking and talking inside, some redoing their hair in the mirror, but the stall at the end was mercifully empty. Nicole slammed into it, locking the door behind her before she broke down, sobbing into the crook of her arm.

She'd never learn. She'd never, ever learn. Why couldn't she forget about Jesse? Why did she keep trying when all it brought her was pain?

She leaned into the door and cried until she'd lost track of time. Then, in one swift, determined gesture, she spun around and forced a finger down her throat, vomiting up the night's junk-food binge in heave after sickening heave.

# Seven

Melanie stood in front of a full-length mirror in her bedroom, making last-minute adjustments to her appearance. Peter would be arriving to pick her up any minute, and she wanted everything to be perfect.

Of course, it was hard to go wrong with the evening gown she'd chosen from her mother's closet. The dress had been Mrs. Andrews's favorite, and Melanie could still remember the almost magical moment that she'd first seen it. She was only a little girl, it was Christmastime, and her parents were going to a benefit of some sort. Her father had been pacing back and forth in the entryway, checking his watch every second.

"Come on, Tristyn," he'd finally shouted up the marble staircase. "We're going to be late!"

And then her mother had appeared on the upstairs landing. Melanie had held her breath, her child's eyes wide as Mrs. Andrews had floated gracefully down the stairs, a thousand sparkling lights flashing from the crystal-studded white fabric of her strapless sheath and the big diamond drops at her ears. Her blond hair had been arranged in curls piled high on her head, the way Melanie's was now, and Melanie remembered thinking she must be the most beautiful woman in the world.

Now Melanie adjusted a curl that had fallen too far forward and wished she'd dared to ask her father for the earrings. The dress had been easy to get— she'd simply walked into her mother's closet and taken it—but the jewels were locked in the safe and Melanie didn't know the combination. The silver-and-crystal substitutes she'd bought at the mall were similar, though, and overall she was pleased.

The doorbell rang. Melanie stiffened with anticipation and took one last look at her image in the mirror, at her wide green eyes, her full pink lips. . . .

"Melanie! Peter's here!" her father called from downstairs.

Grabbing the small beaded clutch that she'd already packed with lipstick, a brush, and breath mints, she hurried to the landing. She could see Peter standing with her father, looking perfectly at ease in a black tuxedo, a wrist corsage in his hands.

It was funny how handsome he was to her now, when she'd barely even noticed him the first time they'd met. That seemed so long ago, and Melanie paused a moment to smile down at him from the top of the stairs. Peter saw her and took a step forward.

"You look . . . unbelievable," he said. "Wow."

Melanie glanced happily from him to her father, hoping for confirmation.

But Mr. Andrews was staring at her with a horrified, stricken expression, as if she were a monster . . . or a ghost.

"Oh, God. Tris," he said, putting a hand to his mouth, and Melanie realized what had happened.

"Dad, I'm sorry!" she cried, hurrying down the stairs to dispel the remnants of that shared memory. "I should have warned you. I should have asked before I borrowed—"

He held up a hand to cut her off. "It's okay. I just never completely realized before how much . . . how . . . never mind." His voice was shaking.

She knew what he'd wanted to say: *how much you look like your mother*. Melanie had noticed that the resemblance was getting stronger, but for the first time it occurred to her how strange that must be for her father—and how painful.

"Thanks," she said softly, stepping off the bottom stair. "I can't think of anyone I'd rather look like."

"Yes. Well." Mr. Andrews looked as if he'd give anything to be locked in his den with a six-pack, but instead he turned to Peter. "I'm trusting you not to drink and drive."

"I never drink, sir," Peter said respectfully. "And I promise to have Melanie home by her curfew."

Melanie laughed at that, and a little of the tension left her body. "*Your* curfew, you mean."

On an impulse, she stretched up on her toes and kissed her father's stubbly cheek. "Good night, Dad."

Mr. Andrews froze, surprised, and then hugged her fiercely, nearly forcing the breath from her lungs. "Be good," he whispered before he released her and rushed out of the entryway.

Melanie finally regained her composure enough to turn to Peter, a wry grin on her face. "Hi. I'll bet that seemed a little weird."

"Maybe not as weird as you think. I believe I got the gist." With a smile of his own, Peter held out a wrist corsage of pale pink baby rosebuds, stretching the elastic for her to slip her hand through.

She did, then held up her wrist to admire it. "It's beautiful. Thank you."

Peter shook his head. "You're beautiful. I feel like an impostor taking you to this thing tonight—you ought to be going with a real date."

"You're crazy," Melanie said, laughing. She wanted to tell him that there wasn't anyone she'd rather go with, that this *was* a real date, but instead she lifted his boutonniere off the hall table. The flower was white, to match her dress, and she pinned it to his lapel as well as she could, suddenly aware of how close to him she was. And the way her fingers were trembling. And how easy it would be to turn her face up to his and kiss him—kiss him as if she meant it this time. . . .

"Well! That's it, I guess. We'd better go," she said, releasing the flower and taking a shaky step backward. If any kissing was going to take place tonight, Peter would have to start it. She'd show that much restraint, at least. Taking a white fur stole from the entry closet, she slipped it over her bare arms and shoulders.

He smiled as he looked her over. "You don't even know how beautiful you are, do you?"

Melanie was used to being complimented, but the obvious sincerity of those simple words nearly moved her to tears. She couldn't help comparing them to the wolf whistles and catcalls most guys she knew seemed to specialize in. More than that, she suspected—no, she knew—that Peter wasn't talking only about what was on the outside. For the first time in her life, she'd met a guy who actually liked her for her.

She linked her arm through his. "Do you know how handsome you are?" she countered.

"Smile!" said the portrait photographer.

No one had to tell Leah to smile. Her lips had been stretched to the limit since the moment she'd walked into the homecoming dance, side by side with Miguel. She snuggled closer to him now, until their cheeks were touching.

A blinding flash went off. "Perfect," the man declared. "That's going to be a nice one."

"It had better be," Miguel said proudly. "My girlfriend's a model, you know." His loud voice carried over the others in that corner of the gym, but for once Leah didn't feel like killing him for mentioning the stupid U.S. Girls contest—not when he'd just called her his girlfriend for the entire school to hear.

"Come on," she said, pulling him away from the makeshift photo studio and out onto the dance floor. "Let's dance—I love this song."

She would have loved any slow song right then, if just for the excuse to feel Miguel's arms around her as they swayed together on the dance floor. Everything about their night to that point had been so incredibly romantic. In the hour that they'd been there, they'd danced only to slow songs, and only with each other. Everyone had seen them. And Miguel looked like a dream in his father's black wedding tuxedo, like the hero in an old-fashioned movie.

"You are so beautiful," he whispered in her ear.

She squeezed him even tighter, remembering the way his eyes had popped when she'd shown up at his house and removed her long black coat so that his mother could take their picture. Her backless floor-length dress was a glossy clinging silk of the richest, deepest red, with halter-style straps connecting to a narrow mandarin collar. To make the most of her bare shoulders, she'd wound her brown hair into a sleek French twist, and there was a hint of smoky shadow around her hazel eyes. Leah had originally planned to buy a strapless gown, but judging by the stunned, nearly stupefied expression its unveiling had left on her boyfriend's face, she had made the right decision when she'd picked the one she was wearing.

Mrs. del Rios had fussed around, trying to find a good place to pose such a tall couple in such a small living room. She had finally settled on a place against an end wall adorned by a carved wooden cross. The cross would definitely be in the pictures, and Leah had half expected Miguel to protest, but he didn't even seem to notice. It was part of the landscape for him by now, she figured, like the framed picture of the Virgin Mary in the kitchen.

"Say fiddlesticks," Mrs. del Rios had directed.

"Fiddlesticks!" Leah had repeated, laughing.

Mrs. del Rios had snapped the picture. Then she'd handed the camera to Rosa and come forward to examine Miguel one last time. "You look so handsome, *mi vida*," she murmured, straightening already straight lapels and fussing with a strand of his dark hair. "You're nearly a man. Your father would be so proud."

Miguel had hemmed and hawed and turned his head away so that no one would see the tears brimming in his brown eyes.

Leah liked Mrs. del Rios. She liked her a lot.

It was horrible to think about how sick she was.

She sighed in Miguel's arms as they made a slow turn on the dance floor. She had been upset with him after dinner Thursday night, when Rosa had spilled the beans about the kidney transplant. It was so like Miguel to keep that from her, to shut her out of his life. Leah had said good-night to Mrs. del Rios and had stalked out to her father's car in a silent fury.

But Miguel had followed on her heels, pleading, explaining, apologizing . . . and she had ultimately forgiven him. After all, it was true that her knowing about it didn't change the situation—it didn't change anything, really. And besides, Mrs. del Rios's illness had been the very last secret between them. She had his solemn word this time.

*It may have been* his *last secret,* she thought guiltily. *But what about yours? You weren't exactly in a hurry to tell him you followed him home and spied on him.*

No, and she wasn't going to, she'd decided. All that was behind them now. Leah just wanted to move forward into the happy new life in front of her—her happy new life with Miguel. It had been a lot of work to arrive at this point in their relationship, but the effort was definitely worth it.

She lifted her head from his shoulder, suddenly reminded of something. "I talked to my parents, and you're invited to dinner Friday night."

"This Friday?" he said, cocking one dark eyebrow. "There's a football game."

"An 'away' game, Miguel. I don't want to drive to Lakeview, do you?"

"Not really," he admitted. "But, hey, isn't that Friday the thirteenth?"

It was. Leah hadn't thought of that.

"Good timing, Rosenthal," he teased. "Way to stack things in my favor."

The song they were dancing to ended, but the two of them stayed on the dance floor, their arms still around each other.

"Friday the thirteenth is only a silly superstition," she told him sweetly. "Standing me up, on the other hand, that's something you *definitely* ought to be afraid of."

Miguel laughed. "Don't worry. I'll be there."

Another song started, a fast one. He looked at her to see what she wanted to do. All around them, couples were splitting up to show off their best dance moves. It looked like fun.

For later.

With a smile, Leah returned her head to his

shoulder, and they resumed slow dancing to a beat only the two of them could hear, the beat of their synchronized hearts.

"Don't you want any popcorn?" Jenna asked, trying to pass the bowl to Nicole. "I feel like I'm eating it all."

She was, and that was fine with Nicole. After the previous night's binge, even the thought of putting those greasy, salty kernels in her mouth made her want to gag. All she could think about were those long, ugly minutes in the girls' room . . . the anger and despair before she'd made herself vomit, the shame and disgust afterward. When she'd been sure the coast was clear, she had slunk from the stall like a criminal, vowing never to do it again. She'd promised that once before, of course, but this time she really meant it. She wanted to be thin—she *would* be thin—but not like that.

"No, you go ahead," she said, pushing the popcorn away.

Jenna ate a little more, then set the half-full bowl on the coffee table in the Brewsters' basement rec room. "I guess I'm not really in the mood either."

Nicole nodded. They both stared blankly at the television screen, where the movie they'd just finished watching was rewinding. If Jenna felt anywhere near as awful as she did, Nicole reflected, then together they felt like the two biggest losers who'd ever slouched on a couch.

"I'll bet they're crowning the homecoming queen about now," Nicole said.

Jenna glanced down at her watch and shrugged. "I guess."

"I wonder who it will be."

"Probably Melanie," Jenna answered, her chin dropping into her chest.

Nicole raised an eyebrow—Jenna was starting to sound as paranoid about Melanie as she was. It was funny, really. Not that long ago, Nicole would have leapt at a chance to trash Melanie behind her back, to say all the nasty, spiteful things she'd been thinking to somebody who could relate. But for some reason, now that the opportunity had arisen, she didn't feel like doing it anymore. She wasn't exactly sure why, but she suspected it had something to do with the fact that Jesse's date for the evening was Vanessa Everyone-Can-Kiss-My-Butt Winters.

"It won't be Melanie," said Nicole. "They'll pick a senior . . . Leah, maybe." That would figure, wouldn't it? Leah had already won the modeling contest that was supposed to launch Nicole's new career *and* hooked up with one of the cutest guys at school—why not become homecoming queen to boot? "My mom was homecoming queen," Nicole added glumly. "That's as close as I'll ever get."

"Don't be so down on yourself," Jenna replied automatically.

Nicole would have liked a little more enthusiasm. Then again, Jenna had problems of her own.

"So who are you more mad at?" Nicole asked. "Peter? Or Melanie?"

The rewinding videotape slammed to a halt, but neither of them made a move to replace it with the second one. Like a genius, Nicole had rented two love stories.

"I'm not mad at Melanie. I *was* mad at Peter," Jenna admitted, "but now I don't know anymore. He tried to make it up to me at the game last night. It's just . . . I'm scared, I guess." She twisted halfway around on the sofa, tucking one stockinged foot beneath her. "I mean, what if he really likes Melanie?"

"Of course he likes her," Nicole answered without thinking. "All the guys like her."

Jenna groaned and let her head fall backward onto the upholstery. "I always took Peter for granted. I totally, totally did. And now I'm losing my best friend."

Nicole made a face. "It's not that bad. Even if he has a crush on Melanie, he'll still be friends with you."

"But not best friends." Jenna seemed incredibly worried. "I never really thought about what would happen if Peter got a girlfriend. He'll have to spend more and more time with her, and after a while I'll hardly see him at all."

"A girlfriend!" Nicole snorted. "Who said anything about a girlfriend?"

"You don't think they'll end up going out?" Jenna asked hopefully.

"No." It was an effort to keep from laughing at the thought. Peter was a nice guy, and Nicole was sure Melanie had some good, private reason for asking him to be her date. But the two of them as a couple? Totally ridiculous. Melanie was so far out of Peter's league that Nicole would be surprised if he could even find the ballpark.

"I doubt anything will come of Jesse and Vanessa, either," Jenna said, apparently trying to return the favor. "I know she's the captain of the cheerleaders and everything, but she never struck me as very nice. It's probably just a one-time thing."

"Yeah? Well . . . the one-timing sucks," Nicole muttered. "I mean, here it is, the first big dance of our junior year, and we're in my basement watching movies. We must be doing *something* wrong."

"I know what you mean," Jenna said slowly. "I've been working on counting my blessings all week—thanking God for my family, our home, Caitlin's new job, and everything else I can think of—and I still feel like a reject. That's got to be wrong of me, don't you think? To feel sorry for myself when God's given me so much?"

"I—I don't know," Nicole stammered. Jenna was asking *her*? Jenna and Peter were always so firm, so enthusiastic, in their faith that Courtney had sarcastically dubbed them the God Squad. If Jenna didn't know, what made her think Nicole would? "I guess I never thought about it like that before."

"But you have to!" Jenna insisted. "Or I do, anyway. When I remember there are kids in the world who are unloved or starving, I feel like the biggest, most ungrateful whiner on earth."

Nicole hesitated. "I probably shouldn't say this, but when I think about *anyone* starving . . . well, it kind of makes me wonder about God at all. You know?"

Jenna's fingers wandered to the cross around her neck. "I know. I don't understand that either. But Jesus said the poor would always be with us, and he also said we could help them anytime. I guess maybe that one is up to us."

"Do you think so? I don't know why God would leave something so important to us." For that matter, Nicole didn't know why God did half the things he did. She *wanted* to know, but those types of questions never seemed to have answers. . . .

The two of them sat there, lost in thought.

"Hey! Can I watch a movie with you guys?"

Heather's loud, obnoxious voice demanded from the stairway behind them.

"No," Nicole answered without turning around. "I told you not to bother us, remember?"

"Yeah, yeah." Heather walked in, picked the bowl of popcorn up off the table, and flopped down on Jenna's end of the couch, stuffing her face. "So what are we watching?"

"I'm warning you, Heather . . . ," Nicole began, but Jenna interceded.

"Oh, let her stay," she said, a wry smile twisting her lips. "It's not like she's crashing a hot date. By the end of an hour with us, she'll probably run out of here screaming anyway."

"Nah. It doesn't usually take that long," Heather quipped, making a face at Nicole.

Nicole knew she ought to kill her. "Whatever," she sighed, getting up to change the tape.

# Eight

Ben hesitated outside the gym, nervously adjusting the jacket of his gray suit—the one he'd worn on Easter and Christmas, when his family had gone to church. He was arriving at the dance very late, but that was all part of his strategy. By now things would be in full gear, couples would be switching around to dance with friends, and everyone would be a lot less likely to notice he was arriving stag.

"Okay, Ben," he whispered. "Let's say it one more time: You're good enough, you're *smart* enough, and people like you."

He'd been repeating that affirmation all day—it was the only thing that had given him the courage to come. That and the killer fan mail posted on the CCHS Web site. Everyone was raving about his new game. Tomb of Terror was a hit! *He* was a hit!

"And that's why no one's going to laugh at you," he promised himself as he pushed the heavy door open. "Just act natural."

No one was bothering to take tickets anymore.

Ben waved his at a chaperone near the door, who nodded for him to come in. In the nearest corner, a photographer was packing up his equipment under a green-and-gold banner that read CCHS HOMECOMING. GO WILDCATS! Ben hadn't been planning to pose for a picture anyway. Instead, he squinted out across the packed dance floor, looking for someone he knew and wishing he'd get used to his stupid new contacts already.

He was still standing there, blinking away, when Angela Maldonado tapped him on the shoulder. Her dress was white chiffon with a sweetheart neckline, and a single strand of pearls bridged the hollow at her throat, cream against her olive skin. Her curly brown hair hung loose, reaching nearly to her waist.

"What are you doing over here by yourself?" she asked. "Where's your date?"

It was the single most dreaded question of the evening. All Ben's positive affirmations were forgotten as his heart thudded a new mantra: *Don't panic, don't panic, don't panic.* "Where's yours?" he countered.

Angela looked put out. "Talking tough with his buddies." She pointed to a group of jocks gathered against the far wall. "I never should have come with a football player."

Ben shrugged, not sure what to say. "You look real nice, though."

"Do you want to dance?" she asked with a smile.

"Uh, yeah. Sure."

*This is almost too easy,* he thought as he followed her onto the dance floor. *My plan is working perfectly!*

Angela was a good dancer, but Ben had been practicing. All that MTV during lonely weekday afternoons was finally paying off. He matched her move for move, then threw in a few more besides. He could feel the glances roaming in their direction. People were starting to notice.

Angela danced closer. "Can I give you some advice?"

"Sure!" he shouted over the music.

"Lose the pirouettes." But she winked at him when she said it, which took away most of the sting.

Okay, so maybe he had gotten a little carried away. He settled down into a more everyday kind of step, focusing on not doing anything stupid like stepping on Angela's feet. It would be just like him to clodhop all over her white satin shoes, or trip her, or slip and fall.

The song came to an end and Angela clapped. Ben wasn't sure if it was for the music or for him, but it made him feel ten feet tall.

"Well, I'd better get back to my date," Angela said with one last smile. "See you in school."

"All right." He watched her walk all the way across the gym before he realized he was standing in the center of the dance floor by himself. Hurriedly he headed for the cover of the refreshment table, where he could plan his next move unobserved.

A cup of punch in hand, Ben surveyed the scene. A couple of people who walked by nodded, as if they actually knew who he was, and a guy from algebra said hello. Ben returned all their greetings but let them go by, not wanting to appear desperate. After a minute, he spotted Leah and Miguel dancing in a corner, then Peter and Melanie talking. He was about to join them when a girl he recognized from third-period civics walked up to the punch bowl with a friend.

*Hey! Don't they have dates?* He wondered if he dared try to capitalize on the situation.

He stole up behind them as they ladled punch into paper cups. "Hi!" he said loudly, startling them into nearly spilling all over their dresses. For a moment, as they stood glaring at him, he almost lost his nerve.

But then he took his courage in hand again. That was the old Ben, the shy, nerdy, glasses-wearing Ben. Tonight he was the much cooler, contact-sporting Benjamin, world-renowned designer of Tomb of Terror! Or someone like that, anyway.

"Sorry to sneak up on you," he apologized smoothly. "But would one of you girls like to dance?"

They looked at him, then each other, as if to assess the alternative. The girl from third period shrugged. "I will," she said, putting down her dripping cup.

Ben danced with her, then her friend, loosening up with every beat of the music and waving to people he recognized in the crowd. After a while he started waving to people he didn't recognize, too, and they actually nodded back. When the girls had danced two songs each, Ben was ready to move on.

"Thanks, ladies," he said, "but I have to get back to my friends." It was better for his image if they thought someone was waiting for him somewhere.

Striking off in the direction he'd last seen Peter, Ben was still edging around the dance floor when the first strains of a ballad filled the gym.

"Jesse!" a girl's voice whined, cutting through the music. "You promised we'd dance a slow song!"

Ben turned to see Jesse and Vanessa Winters sitting in two of the folding chairs lining the poorly lit wall.

"Come on, you've rested long enough." She pulled Jesse onto his feet and dragged him toward the dance floor.

"Hi, Jesse," Ben said as they passed.

"Hey, Ben."

Ben hadn't known Jesse was bringing Vanessa to the dance, but he wasn't that surprised. He could have guessed Jesse would go for someone like her—someone who looked good on paper. From the expression on Jesse's face as he went by, though, Ben

123

had a feeling the guy was adding up his columns again and finding himself in the red anyway.

When Ben finally caught up with Melanie and Peter, they were standing beneath a clump of green and yellow balloons.

"Ben! Great to see you!" Peter said. "You made it after all!"

The greeting took Ben aback. Peter had to be referring to the fact that Jenna had turned him down for a date. Ben had managed not to think about Jenna's lie for a couple of days, and it didn't feel great to be reminded of it by the guy she was supposed to be there with. *Where is Jenna, anyway?* he wondered.

"You're here right on time, buddy," Peter continued, "because I definitely need to excuse myself." He glanced in the direction of the rest rooms by way of explanation. "Keep Melanie company until I get back, all right?" He was off before Ben could answer.

"Hi, Melanie," said Ben, feeling suddenly awkward. He was never really sure if Melanie liked him or not. "That's a pretty dress."

She smiled—that dazzling cheerleader smile of hers—and the low lights sparkled in the diamonds at her ears. Ben knew that half the guys in the room were probably watching him at that moment.

"Do you want to dance?" he blurted out; then his eyes went wide with alarm. What was he thinking? This wasn't an Eight Prime meeting in Peter's living room; it was the homecoming formal in front of the entire school. And it was still a slow song!

"I mean, uh, you don't have to," he added hastily, wishing he'd never mentioned it.

Melanie looked surprised, but she smiled again and shrugged her suntanned shoulders. "Sure. Why not?"

He held her gingerly on the dance floor, being careful—*so* careful—not to step on anything, and understood for a few brief minutes what it felt like to be cool. All the girls around them threw envious glances at Melanie, wanting to be her no matter who she was dancing with, and all the guys . . . all the guys wanted to be him. Ben was sure of it. The song came to an end and he released her quickly, relieved that his hands weren't sweating.

They talked while they waited for Peter.

"What do you think about Brooke Henderson being named homecoming queen?" Melanie asked him. "Nobody saw that coming."

Least of all Ben. He hadn't even been there. "I don't know."

"I'm happy for her. It's about time it was won by someone besides a cheerleader." Melanie's eyes were focused on the dance floor as she spoke, and Ben noticed Jesse and Vanessa in that general area.

"Well, it's not like Brooke is a nobody," he said. "She *is* the senior class president."

Then Peter returned to dance with Melanie, and Ben went for more punch. He was filling his cup when he heard two of the sounds he dreaded most—Mitch Powell's voice and Whitey Wallace's laugh—behind him. He froze, his pulse pounding. Then, slowly, he lowered the ladle back into the punch bowl and turned to face the dance floor.

The pair was standing right in front of him.

"Uh, hi, guys," Ben said weakly. They wouldn't beat him up in front of everyone. Would they? He braced himself for whatever was coming.

"Saw you dancing with Melanie Andrews," said Mitch.

"Oh, yeah? She's a good friend," Ben said nervously.

They looked surprised.

"Saw your computer game," Whitey drawled.

Ben wouldn't have thought Whitey had the mental wherewithal to plug in a computer, much less play Tomb of Terror, but he nodded, hoping his smile didn't reveal how afraid he was.

The three of them stood looking at each other for a long, uncomfortable moment.

"See you around, Pipkin," Mitch said finally.

"See ya," Whitey echoed.

Ben watched them walk off, then tossed down his punch in one gulp.

They didn't want to harass him anymore.

He'd arrived!

"Okay," the deejay announced from the dais at the end of the gym. "This is the last set of songs, so let's see everyone out there dancing."

Melanie and Peter were already on the floor when Leah and Miguel joined them.

"Hi!" Leah called, waving and dancing alongside.

Melanie smiled and waved back. She'd seen Leah and Miguel a few other times that night, but for the most part they'd been sticking close together, keeping to the fringes where the light was low. Melanie could understand that completely.

What she *couldn't* understand was Jesse and Vanessa. And it was going to drive her crazy.

All evening long, even though she was having a great time with Peter, Melanie had been obsessing over that strange couple. What was Jesse trying to pull, anyway? He couldn't really like Vanessa. Could he?

And Vanessa! Instead of being upset about not getting homecoming queen, she'd been totally gracious, congratulating Brooke and cheering along with the crowd. It was unnatural.

Melanie cast another furtive glance to where they were dancing, the way she'd been doing for hours. Unfortunately, this time Vanessa caught her. And rather than ignoring Melanie or simply smiling, she waved, grabbed Jesse by the wrist, and started dragging him over.

*Great*, Melanie thought sarcastically. *Super*.

The last thing she wanted was to have her last few dances with Peter ruined by Jesse and stuck-up Vanessa. Still . . . she couldn't deny that she was curious to see those two in action.

"Hi, Melanie!" Vanessa stopped only inches away and pulled Jesse up beside her. "Isn't this fun?" She shimmied her shoulders as if excited, setting the beaded fringe on her black dress swaying.

Melanie stopped dancing and shouted over the music. "Vanessa, this is Peter Altmann. Peter, Vanessa Winters." She turned to introduce Miguel and Leah, but found they'd disappeared again.

Peter smiled and extended his hand to Vanessa. She just smirked and nodded, too impolite to loosen her grip on Jesse for even a second.

Far from seeming pleased by his date's attention, however, Jesse looked as though he could barely keep his ultrasuave smile plastered to his face. Melanie was reminded of a big, wild dog on a short, short leash.

"Having a good time, Jesse?" she couldn't resist asking. It was the first time she'd spoken to him directly since he'd tried to drop out of Eight Prime.

"Of course." He threw an arm across Vanessa's shoulders and cranked up the smile a notch. "Why wouldn't I be?"

Vanessa beamed.

Melanie could think of several reasons—starting with the fact that Vanessa was clearly bossing him around the way she did everyone else—but she choked them all back. She didn't like Vanessa, but she didn't hate her either. She was certainly good enough for Jesse.

"I love your dress," Vanessa offered.

"Thanks." But there was something so smarmy about Vanessa's smile that Melanie wasn't sure whether to believe her or not. It was that *look*, that don't-you-envy-me, I've-beaten-you-at-your-own-game look.

"So, how's it going, Peter?" Jesse asked. "Didn't Jenna come?"

Melanie's attention was ripped from Vanessa by the sudden urge to kick Jesse in the shin. Jenna's name had been hanging in the air between her and Peter all night, and now here was stupid Jesse, bringing it up again.

*He must have known Peter and I were coming together*, she thought. But then she reconsidered. She certainly hadn't told him. Perhaps he was even more surprised to see her with Peter than she was to see him with Vanessa.

"No. She, uh . . . didn't want to," Peter replied.

"I didn't expect you to come tonight either," Melanie told Jesse, eager to change the subject.

He gave her a sharp look and tightened his grip

on Vanessa's shoulders. "I probably wouldn't have, if Vanessa hadn't come with me. She was the only person I really wanted to go with."

Vanessa shot Melanie a jubilant look, as if she'd just won something. "You knew I'd go with you," she teased her date in a nauseatingly coy voice. "I don't go up to the lake with just anyone."

*The lake?* Melanie felt as if she'd been hit in the gut, but she wasn't sure why.

Jesse looked annoyed. "It was just one time last summer. I don't think we need to tell everyone, Vee."

Vanessa tossed Melanie that weird look again.

*No, not everyone,* Melanie realized. *Just me. She wants me to know.*

But if she hadn't just heard it from them, Melanie wouldn't have believed it. Jesse had had a summer fling with Vanessa? And neither of them had ever mentioned it to her? On the contrary, they always acted as if they barely knew each other. The only time Vanessa ever spoke of Jesse was to say what a slimy flirt he was, and Melanie couldn't remember hearing Jesse ever speak of Vanessa at all. In fact, he'd been so insistent in his pursuit of Melanie that she'd never guessed there was anyone else. . . .

None of it made any sense.

Except maybe Vanessa's snotty attitude toward her. When Melanie had made the cheerleading squad in the spring, Vanessa had seemed genuinely happy to have her on board, but over the summer she'd become aloof, and in the fall things had turned downright chilly. If she'd been carrying a torch for Jesse over some half-baked summer romance, that could explain a lot. How it must have killed her to see him following Melanie like a second shadow, especially since his efforts got him nowhere.

And then there was the way Vanessa was always baiting her about Jesse. Always trying to make Melanie say she liked him when she didn't. Trying to get a rise out of her before the homecoming game by announcing plans to go out with him. Trying to get a reaction just now with her pathetic revelation about the two of them at the lake. . . .

*Like I care!* If Jesse was the source of all Vanessa's attitude toward her, then the girl had even bigger problems than Melanie had given her credit for.

"This one's for the ladies," the deejay announced, breaking into the music in a smooth, cool voice. "I know all you girls want one last dance with that special someone." He keyed up a romantic song, and couples everywhere melted into each other.

"I want to dance this," Melanie told Peter, tugging on his hand to put some distance between them and Vanessa.

"Yeah, me too." They moved to a less crowded

area and Peter opened his arms. Melanie stepped inside their safe circle, putting her hands behind his neck and laying her head on his shoulder. All she wanted was to savor the moment, to forget about everything else. But as Peter turned her slowly to the music, she found herself face-to-face with Vanessa again.

Vanessa had wriggled into Jesse's arms; her body was pressed tightly to his. She peered over his shoulder at Melanie now, her eyes half closed with exaggerated bliss.

*I'll bet she's had it in for me all along*, Melanie realized suddenly. *Making me cook at the carnival with Jesse . . . not telling me when she thought he cheated with Nicole . . . I'll bet she was glad when I got hurt. For all I know, that was the point of that whole stupid trick.*

The possibility actually made her miss a step, but Peter's arms held her up, getting her gently back on the beat.

*No, that's ridiculous. Even Vanessa wouldn't stoop that low.*

Still, she clearly thought of Jesse as her property. And tonight she seemed to be declaring it for all the world to see—the world and Melanie Andrews.

Melanie shook her head against Peter's tuxedoed shoulder. The whole thing was so stupid—Vanessa could have him! She could have *always* had him.

Assuming she could hang on to him. Because

Melanie knew Jesse. She knew him better than she wanted to. And by the look in his eyes tonight . . .

*He'll dump her. He'll dump her hard.*

*And Vanessa will blame me.*

"Well, I guess this is good night, then," Jesse said, pulling his car to a stop in front of Vanessa's house. "Um, thanks for a great time, Vee."

"I love it when you call me Vee," she said, making no move to get out.

"You do?" He had seriously miscalculated, then. His twelve-year-old stepsister, Brittany, hated it when he called her Bee.

"I don't know why you had to bring me home so early, though," she complained.

"It's not early, Vanessa. We stayed till the end of the dance."

"So. Can't you think of anything you want to do with me now?" she asked coyly.

Nothing she'd want to hear about. Jesse was certain of that.

But she was already leaning toward him, puckering up, and Jesse knew he at least had to kiss her good night. There was no way out of that unless he wanted a scene. And he didn't. He just wanted to get away from her. Far, far away.

He kissed her, thinking of Melanie in Peter Altmann's arms, Melanie in his arms. . . .

133

"All right!" he said, breaking things off abruptly. "Well, I guess I'll see you around."

Before Vanessa could protest, he was out his door and around the car, already opening hers. It was nearly freezing outside, which was perfect. No one could expect prolonged good-byes in this kind of dismal weather.

"What do you mean, you'll see me around? When?" she asked as he almost trotted her up her walkway.

"Well . . . I'll see you at school on Monday."

"That wasn't what I meant." Her tone was irritated, and there was just a hint of hardening around her close-set eyes.

"Well, geez, Vanessa. I don't know. I'll call you."

"When will you call me?"

*When hell freezes over. When pigs sprout wings. When you stop acting like you own me. . . .*

"Soon. Sometime soon, all right?"

That seemed to satisfy her, and with one last kiss, he was able to get away.

"What a mistake!" he groaned as he pointed his BMW toward home. "What a stupid mistake."

Asking Vanessa to the dance had been a disaster from the start. He'd already known he didn't like her—he'd just needed someone high enough up the social scale to bolster his sinking reputation. And somehow he'd had a feeling that the captain of the cheerleading squad would be happy to oblige.

She'd been too happy, though—that was the problem. She'd never even told him she already had a date with Ricky Black. He'd had to get the news about her breaking that off from a couple of Ricky's teammates. So now the basketball team was mad at him in addition to the football team, and it was all his own dumb fault. He should have guessed she'd be going with *someone*, since he'd waited until Thursday to ask her.

Jesse steered around a turn, his tires squealing. It wasn't as if he hadn't paid the price, though. For the last two days Vanessa had been totally obnoxious. She'd made him come to the bonfire on Friday, and then she'd spent the evening hanging all over him, acting like his girlfriend and obviously expecting far, far more than he had any intention of giving her. It was almost enough to make him wish he'd made a date with Nicole after all.

Then again, he'd think twice before he listened to any more of her bright ideas—she was the one who'd talked him into going to the dance in the first place. And despite Nicole's theory, none of the guys on the team who were supposed to notice him there with Vanessa had paid the least bit of attention. They'd all given him the cold shoulder, pretending to be into their dates. Or maybe they really were—who knew? He must have had rocks in his head to let Nicole convince him a formal could be a male bonding experience.

"What a total waste," he muttered disgustedly. And he could only imagine what this second breakup with Vanessa was going to cost him. He'd never promised her anything, never asked her for more than a date to the dance, but somehow she'd expanded that simple invitation into this whole big relationship that only existed in her head. The way she'd acted in front of Peter and Melanie was nothing short of embarrassing.

*Well, she'll get the picture when I don't call her,* he thought. At least he hoped she would.

He flipped on the radio and scanned through the stations, eager to distract himself. Country, country, gospel, country. He put in a rock CD and turned up the volume. It was at times like these that he missed California the most. It was strange how such stupid little things, like no decent radio stations, could make him feel like a foreigner in his own country.

He sighed, wondering if his life would ever get back to normal—or even to the semi-acceptable state he'd come to accept as normal in Missouri. *At least on Monday Coach Davis is supposed to tell me if I can play again or not,* he thought, anxious for that limbo to end. It wasn't much to look forward to, but it was starting to feel like all he had.

He pulled into his driveway and hit the button on his garage door opener, parking in the three-car garage. Then, leaning back in his seat, he reached down under the passenger seat and retrieved a beach-towel–wrapped bundle. Lifting it carefully into his lap, he gently unwound the towel. The un-opened bottle of vodka it contained glittered in the half darkness inside the car.

It hadn't been easy to get. He'd had to drive all the way out to the university, where he'd hung around a liquor store until he'd seen what he was looking for: a bunch of older frat guys on their way up to the door. With a sob story about the big dance that night and the price of a twelve-pack as a bribe, Jesse hadn't had much trouble convincing them to add the vodka to their shopping list.

All afternoon it had been under his seat, and all that evening, too. Jesse fingered the paper seal now, eager to break it open. He was just about to do it when, for some reason, he remembered Melanie and Coach Davis both saying he had a drinking problem. He hesitated, wondering if by any remote chance . . .

*No. Ridiculous*, he scoffed. *If I really had a prob-lem, wouldn't this bottle be half gone already? I could have opened it hours ago and been taking shots all day.* It certainly would have made his time with Vanessa more pleasant. But he hadn't done it. And why?

*Well, mostly because I didn't trust her not to rat me out*, he admitted. But also because he didn't have any desire to wrap his BMW around a tree. He wasn't an idiot; he picked his times and places. That alone ought to prove there wasn't a problem.

He started to twist off the cap, then forced himself to stop. *No, I'll sneak it up to my bedroom,* he decided, tucking it inside his coat. *Everyone's asleep by now. I can drink until I pass out cold and no one will ever know.*

After the night he'd had, he could barely wait.

# Nine

"Mom? Dad?" Leah stumbled out into the living room, still wearing her pajamas even though it was almost eleven o'clock Sunday morning. She'd slept like a stone—she still wasn't fully awake.

On the dining room table she found a croissant and a note: *Gone shopping. Home soon. M & D.*

"Great," she grumbled, pulling up a chair. They'd been sleeping when she'd come home the night before, and she wanted to tell them about the dance.

*Oh, well, they'll be back eventually.* In the meantime, she was starving. Breaking up the croissant, she began slathering the pieces with butter and raspberry jam.

From the table, she could see that the coffee-maker on the kitchen counter still held half a pot. She got up to pour herself a mug, then gathered the scattered sections of the Sunday paper and took them back to her chair, flipping idly through their pages as she ate.

She was supposed to write a mock letter to the

editor of *The Clearwater Herald* as homework for her journalism class, and the assignment was due on Monday. It should have been an easy task, but Leah couldn't think of a topic. As far as she could tell, people usually wrote to the editor about their pet peeves, and she couldn't think of a peeve of hers that anyone else would care about.

She read the arts section and all the book and movie reviews before she turned with a sigh to that day's letters to the editor, hoping that maybe this time someone had written something that would give her an idea. But, as usual, the burning issues of Clearwater Crossing weren't particularly inspiring. One woman had written in to complain about people who let their cats do their business in other people's flower beds—she thought all cats ought to be on leashes. The second writer complained of a broken parking meter downtown that had resulted in his getting a supposedly undeserved ticket. To hear the author tell it, the police not only *knew* the meter was broken, they'd *installed* it that way, as a conspiracy against innocent citizens.

"Par-a-noid!" Leah sang under her breath.

There was only one letter left.

*Dear Editor:*

*For months I have looked the other way, minded my own business, and kept my mouth shut. But I must finally speak out about the* shameful budget priorities of our city council. These elected officials, who are supposed to be safeguarding the interests of the majority, think no further than their own petty interests and convenience, and the way they waste tax dollars is a travesty.

For example, Councilman Nash spent two weeks in Washington, D.C., this summer, at taxpayer expense, "lobbying for our interests." If that isn't ridiculous enough, his wife and three school-age children went with him, also at taxpayer expense.

Our council members routinely charge all their meals and parking expenses to the city, whether they're related to city business or not. And has anyone noticed the council's automobiles lately? All new, all leased, all paid for by us.

These little perks add up to big money—money that has to be found somewhere else in an already tight budget—and I, for one, am sick of it. Maybe some of you have noticed that potholes aren't being fixed, our schools need painting, and our libraries need new books. Or you may have read about Eight Prime, eight local teens who are earning a bus the city had previously pledged to buy for an underprivileged children's program.

Where did the budgeted money for that bus go? All I know is that the city council just had new covered parking built at city hall for its *exclusive use. And that project wasn't in the budget.*

*But don't take my word for it. I challenge all who read this letter to check the facts themselves. Pressure must be put on the council to change its ways and to remember the money it is spending is ours!*

A City Insider Who's Seen Too Much

Leah was on the edge of her chair by the time she read the final paragraphs. This was a bombshell! Everyone was going to be talking about it.

"I have to call Peter," she said, heading for the telephone with the newspaper clutched in her hand. "There's got to be some way we can turn this to our advantage."

She looked up Peter's number and dialed it hurriedly. The phone rang and rang, but no one answered.

*He ought to be back from church by now!* she thought, glancing anxiously at the kitchen clock. An answering machine finally picked up.

"The Altmanns are not at home," said the recorded voice. "Please leave your name, number, and—"

"Yeah, yeah, yeah," Leah muttered impatiently. "Get to the beep already."

The moment it sounded, she blurted out her message.

"Peter? This is Leah. Listen, something important's come up. Call me the second you get in, all right?"

"Peter, what are you doing here?" Jenna asked, opening her front door wider.

When she'd seen him at church that morning, he hadn't said a thing about coming to her house. Not that they'd exchanged enough words after the service to call it a conversation. The cold front that had been moving over the state for the last few days seemed to have gotten stuck, and Jenna had used the excuse to rush to her father's warm van. She hadn't even asked Peter if he had enjoyed himself at the dance. She didn't want to know anyway.

Peter smiled. "I thought we could go on a picnic."

"Today?" Jenna protested. "Now? It's freezing out there."

"So we'll take my car instead of the bikes. Come on, I packed a killer lunch."

"I don't know. . . ." Jenna stalled. A Sunday picnic with Peter had always been one of her favorite things. She'd lost track of the number of times they'd pedaled their bicycles along the dirt and gravel trails to the picnic tree with the tire swing, but she had only to close her eyes to feel the sun on her shoulders and the wind in her face, to hear the gravel crunching beneath her tires, to smell the dust on the road, and to see the brilliant green canopy of leaves arching over their plaid blanket. She didn't want to taint those precious memories with a cold, car-bound picnic on a sullen day.

But Peter was insistent. "My mom made cookies," he tempted her. "Chocolate chip."

He knew those were her favorite, and the way Mrs. Altmann made them was especially good, with shaved chocolate and finely chopped nuts. Still, Jenna wasn't a child, to be bought off with desserts.

"She made them just for you," Peter wheedled. "If you don't eat them she'll be crushed."

"Fine." Jenna relented, even as she wondered how much of that story was true. Peter never lied, but he had been known to exaggerate. "Just let me get my coat and tell my mom where I'm going. By the way, where *am* I going? We can't drive to the tree."

"You'll see," he said mysteriously, leaving Jenna to simply tell her mother she was going to lunch with Peter.

They didn't talk much on the way. Jenna wasn't sure what to say. She wasn't mad anymore, but she was still hurt. More than that, she was confused— about Peter's feelings for Melanie, about what it might mean to their friendship. It was an awkward ride, with so many things unspoken between them. Jenna could feel the weight of the words hanging in the air, fogging the edges of the windows.

At last Peter turned down the dirt road to the lake and pulled into the deserted parking lot. A cold wind ruffled the dark green water, but otherwise all was quiet.

"How's this?" he asked. "We've got a nice view and we don't even have to get out of the car."

Jenna didn't bother to mention the obvious—that the lake was the school make-out spot. She knew nothing like that had crossed Peter's mind.

"It's fine."

Peter was already unloading a cardboard box he'd retrieved from the backseat. "This is for your lap," he told her, handing her a large cloth napkin. "Think of it as a miniature picnic blanket." Then he pulled out paper plates and plastic forks, two thick roast beef sandwiches on homemade bread, twin containers of fruit salad, and a foil-covered plate full of cookies. "Soda or juice?" he asked, holding up a drink in each hand.

The elaborateness of Peter's preparations was starting to make her feel like an idiot for worrying about coming. "You really went all out," she murmured, reaching for the juice.

"Nothing's too good for my best friend. Oops, I almost forgot the soup!" He pulled a Thermos from behind her seat and unscrewed the lid, allowing a curl of steam to escape in the car. "Potato. You like that, right?" Potato was her favorite. He handed her a Styrofoam cup and filled it with creamy white soup. "You can set that on the dashboard if you want."

It was too hot to eat, so Jenna took his advice and began with her sandwich instead. They ate awhile in silence, but it was no longer the nervous, uncertain silence of that morning. Jenna was starting to understand that Peter's painstaking picnic preparations said more about the state of their friendship than words ever could. They were fine. They were still friends. Nothing could ever change that.

"Good sandwich," she said, polishing off the last bite and starting on the fruit.

"Thanks." Peter smiled, and Jenna felt as if she'd come home.

At last the too-large lunch was finished, and the trash, dishes, and empty Thermos were packed away in the box. They tilted their car seats back and gazed at the empty lake.

"You know, Jenna," said Peter, finally getting to the subject that no longer seemed so urgent, "I really am sorry about last night."

"Yeah, me too. I'm sorry I was such a baby, I mean. Did you and Melanie have fun?"

"We did. But it wasn't the same without you. I kept wondering what you were doing, wishing you had come."

"Really?"

Peter smiled and nodded. "I have something for you," he said, reaching over to pop open his glove compartment. Inside was a bundle the size of a soda can, wrapped in the Sunday comics and sporting a half-crushed pink bow. He fished it out and handed it to her. "Here."

"Gee, I hate to wreck such gorgeous gift wrap," Jenna teased, but she was burning with curiosity. The package was moderately heavy for its size, and she could feel irregular contours through the paper.

"Just open it," Peter said, laughing.

She prolonged the suspense for one more minute, then ripped off the paper in one rushed motion.

"So? What do you think?"

But Jenna couldn't speak for the sudden lump in her throat. She couldn't look at him, either, afraid he'd see the tears that blurred her vision. The gift she held in her hands was a ceramic statuette of two little kids—a blond boy and a brown-haired girl—hugging in front of an old tree trunk. Their feet were far apart but their faces were cheek to jaw, and their pudgy arms stretched to close the distance. On the circular base were inscribed two words:

**BEST FRIENDS**

"Did I mention that I'm also really sorry I gave you such a hard time about the whole Miguel thing?" Peter said anxiously, apparently worried by her lack of a reply. "Let's just put everything behind us, can we?"

Jenna still couldn't answer, but she did the best she could. She put her arms around him and pressed her cheek to his. Their bodies were far apart, but their arms stretched to close the distance.

"I can," she finally managed.

# *Ten*

When Leah stepped out of the main building after school on Monday, she saw a flock of students gathered around a white van parked on the access road through the school grounds. Rarely was there anything other than a cafeteria delivery truck on that pavement, and Leah hurried down to join the crowd, wondering what was going on.

She wove and jostled her way to the front, then stopped short in surprise. The van was from the local news station, and a television reporter was talking to Peter and Jenna in front of it!

*This has got to be about that letter to the editor,* Leah thought, running out to join her friends. When Peter had finally returned her call the afternoon before, they had discussed trying to capitalize on it in some way, but they hadn't come up with a plan. Now it appeared that he and Jenna had figured one out on their own.

"Hi! What's going on?" Leah whispered to Jenna as the reporter continued to talk with Peter. "Are they doing a story about the bus?"

149

"About the city council," Jenna whispered back. "They're trying to figure out exactly what those guys promised Peter."

"But how did they find him here?" Leah asked.

Jenna smiled. "I sent them an e-mail last night and told them where we'd be, just in case they wanted to talk to us. When we came out of the building, here they were."

"E-mail! Why didn't I think of that?"

The reporter broke off her discussion with Peter to give Leah a keep-it-down look. Then she turned to a guy standing near the van. "Okay, Tony. We're ready to go on camera here. This won't take long— just a quick statement."

Tony grabbed his camera while the reporter positioned Peter with his back toward the main façade of the high school. Leah and Jenna were motioned out of the shot.

"Ready?" the reporter asked. Tony started filming, and the interview began.

"This is Tammy Winfred reporting from Clearwater Crossing High School, where I'm speaking with Peter Altmann," she said in an on-camera voice. "Peter, we understand that the city council reneged on funds it had promised your park program for a vehicle, then spent those funds on covered parking spaces. Can you comment?"

Peter nodded. "We were promised a bus for the Junior Explorers program at Clearwater Crossing

Park. I don't know exactly how much money was earmarked for that, but in September they told us the money wasn't there after all."

"And that they'd spent it on parking instead?"

Peter laughed. "Well, actually they spoke to my partner, Chris, not to me, but I'm pretty sure they didn't tell him that."

"But surely they must have given you *some* explanation," the reporter pressed, determined to get a damaging sound bite.

"Just that it wasn't in the budget." Then, as Leah and Jenna watched, Peter seized the moment. "But that doesn't mean we've given up. A group of us are earning that bus ourselves. We've already made almost six thousand dollars, and we've got a bus all picked out. If we could get even a little help, it would be great."

"Help from the city council, you mean?"

Peter shrugged. "Or whoever wants to donate to a very worthy cause. In fact, if people watching want to help, they can send any size donation to my church, care of . . . uh, care of the Junior Explorers Bus Fund," he improvised, giving the church's address. "I give my word that every penny collected will go for the bus, and not to, uh, any other project," he added, with a trace of an ironic smile.

"All right. Thank you, Peter," said Tammy, motioning for Tony to stop taping. As soon as the camera was off, her voice returned to normal.

"Well, good luck," she said, shaking Peter's hand. "I hope you get your bus."

Leah and Jenna hurried over to join them.

"When are you going to run that interview?" Leah asked Tammy. "I want to be sure to see it."

"It ought to be on sometime tonight." The reporter climbed into the van and the news crew drove away.

"Wow, Peter, great thinking!" Jenna congratulated him as the crowd of spectators dissolved. "I didn't know you were going to ask people to send donations to church."

Peter glanced skyward, then smiled at the two girls. "Neither did I."


Jesse noticed the crowd around the van as he headed to the gym, but he didn't have time to investigate. He was supposed to meet Coach Davis before practice, and with everything on the line, he didn't dare be late. This was the day the coach was supposed to tell him whether he'd play with the team again.

A few guys were already dressing in the locker room when Jesse walked in. He checked his watch anxiously, then ran the final few yards to the coach's office. Coach Davis was waiting in his desk chair, going over some paperwork.

"Jones!" he said as Jesse walked in. "You remembered."

Jesse nodded. What did the guy think? That he was going to forget an appointment this important? He had the feeling Coach Davis was toying with him, that he'd been toying with him for weeks, and the game was getting old. As he took a seat across the desk, Jesse worked to keep his dislike from showing, but his opinion of the coach had suffered a lot and was still sliding steadily downward. He waited in silence to hear his fate pronounced.

"So how's the drinking going?" asked the coach. "Have you quit?"

"Yes, sir, I have." Jesse had expected the lie to be more difficult, especially after the bender he'd indulged in over the weekend, but it slid from his lips with amazing ease, ringing with false truth. *After all*, he told himself, *what I do on my own time is none of the coach's business. Just because he caught me making one stupid mistake, it doesn't mean he owns me. It's his fault I had to lie.*

Coach Davis smiled, satisfied. "I thought so. You seem to be paying more attention on the field. I see traces of the old star shining through again."

Once, the compliment would have meant everything. Now Jesse had to concentrate on keeping the smirk off his face. The coach had bought it!

"Thank you, sir," he said, amazed by how humble he sounded. He was getting good at this.

"All right, Jones. You can play in the Lakeview

game this Friday. I know you've been working hard to prove yourself, and you still have a ways to go, but I'm happy to see you turning things around. I'll tell you the truth: I always thought you would."

Coach had believed in him all along? He certainly hadn't shown it. But it didn't matter now—Jesse was back on the team!

"Well, uh, thanks," he said, smiling with relief. "Football is my top priority. I'll work harder still, if that's what it takes."

The coach made a dismissive gesture. "Sure, football's important. But not as important as character. Not as important as a man's word. If a man gives his word, you ought to be able to trust him. I wasn't talking just now about the way you've been playing. I meant I had a feeling you'd keep your promise about not drinking, and I'm glad you did."

"Oh." All the superiority Jesse had felt at fooling the coach evaporated in an instant. Suddenly he felt kind of guilty. His pleasure at being back on the team was tainted by the knowledge that he wasn't who the coach thought he was—he wasn't a man of his word.

"Okay," Coach Davis said. "You'd better hurry and get suited up, so let me just give you your community service project and you'll be on your way."

"What?"

The coach shuffled some papers, found the one he was looking for, and passed it over the desk to

Jesse. "You'll be helping an elderly gentleman named Charlie Johnson with some chores around the house. Cleaning, yard work, errands—that type of thing. He lives alone, and it's getting harder for him to do things himself."

"Who said anything about community service?" Jesse protested. "You never mentioned that before!"

The coach looked unpleasantly surprised as he slowly retracted the paperwork. "Are you saying you won't do it?" he asked, a touch of ice in his voice. His demeanor had changed completely, and Jesse had to admit that he was still a little scared of the guy.

"No," Jesse said, backpedaling quickly. "It's just that I'm really busy and, and . . . why can't I count Eight Prime? I'm already doing charity."

"Which is one of the very few things that saved your butt. Look, Jones, it's forty hours of community service. That's the rule, and I don't think it's too much to ask. Not only that, but I got you what I thought was a good assignment. If you don't want it, though . . ." The coach let the sentence trail off, but it was obvious from his tone that the consequences weren't worth considering.

"I didn't say I wouldn't do it," Jesse grumbled, pulling the paper out of the coach's hand. *Charlie Johnson, 435 West Rockford Street*, he read silently. He had no idea where that was. There was a telephone number and some directions, though. He supposed he'd figure it out. *Just what I need*, he thought irritably. *Another charity project.*

"They're going to check, you know," said the coach. "The agency that phoned in the assignment will check to see if you're doing it."

"Fine! I said I'm doing it!"

Coach Davis gave him a long, hard look. "Go suit up."

"Ben!"

Ben hesitated, then turned to see who had called him. He'd been late getting out of class, and there were few people left in the hall. A blond guy in jeans and a ski jacket waved and hurried over.

"Hi. I'm Mark Foster," he said. "You don't know me, but I recognize you from your picture on Tomb of Terror. What a cool game."

Ben smiled proudly. "Thank you."

"Hey, I was wondering if you could help me out with a problem I'm having on the fourth level, though."

"I could, but don't you want to figure it out yourself?"

Mark grimaced slightly. "It's not that kind of problem. My computer keeps crashing."

"Crashing?"

"You know that secret door at the end of the eastern corridor?"

Ben nodded. The mummy had guarded that door.

"Well, every time I step through it, my computer locks up completely. I have to reboot to get out."

"That shouldn't be happening," Ben said apprehensively. "What kind of hardware are you running? Are you sure you have enough RAM?"

The two of them ran through the specs on Mark's computer, which were more than adequate to run the game.

"I don't know why you're having a problem," Ben admitted. "But I'll look into it when I get home."

Mark nodded. "Okay. So I'll see you around, then."

"Yeah. See ya."

But on the bus on the way home, Ben became more and more worried. Instead of noticing how his plan had just succeeded in bringing him another potential friend, he obsessed about what could be making Mark's computer lock up. He might have been calmer if the problem hadn't occurred near an area he'd worked on, but that little coincidence made him almost too frightened to think.

The moment the bus dropped him off, Ben ran to his room and launched the game, maneuvering straight to the fourth level. *So far, so good*, he thought as he approached the secret door. The heavy stone slid away. He was crouching in front of the opening . . . he was stepping through it . . . he was stuck. The game froze with his character barely inside the secret passageway and refused to respond to commands. His computer had locked up.

*This is bad.* His heart was pounding and his breathing had grown shallow. *This is really bad.*

Ben rebooted his machine and opened the code for the secret door. He didn't see anything wrong, but when he tried the door again, his computer locked up again. Feeling slightly sick to his stomach, he rebooted and logged onto the CCHS Web site to check the guest book. Sure enough, he had four angry e-mail messages, all complaining about the same thing.

"Stay calm," he told himself under his breath. "This is only a little snag. You'll get it fixed. Besides, people don't even need to be on the fourth level to win."

It was amazing how unreassured he felt. *Come on, now, Ben. You're good enough, you're smart enough, and—*

"If you don't figure this out, you're dead," he finished aloud.

He looked at the code once more and *still* didn't see anything wrong. Crossing his fingers, he launched the game and tried the secret door again. The exact same thing happened.

*Dad would spot the problem in a heartbeat,* he thought. He imagined his father clicking through the code, making everything right. He was so good at things like that. But how could Ben ask his dad to help him when he wasn't even supposed to have the game, let alone have posted it on the Internet?

*I'll run a virus scan,* he decided, not sure what that would accomplish. He only knew he had to do something. He clicked the icon to launch the program and watched as the opening screen came up. But halfway through the launch, an error message posted in the center of the screen.

"What do you mean, you can't find the file?" Ben argued with the monitor. "It's right there, right where it's always been."

But the program refused to launch, and Ben was starting to sweat in earnest.

"What the heck is going on? Come on, you stupid thing, work!"

# Eleven

Leah peered out the streaming window of Burger City at the rain coming down in the parking lot. "We picked a bad day to eat lunch off campus," she said, turning to Miguel. "I really thought we'd make it back before those clouds let loose."

Miguel smiled. "I told you," he said, with great satisfaction.

Leah twirled the whoopee signal with a long french fry.

"My mom's making lasagna for dinner Friday night," she said, changing the subject. "You like lasagna, right? Because if you don't, there's still time to ask her to change it."

"It's only Tuesday," Miguel protested. "I can't believe you're worried about what we're eating on Friday."

"I knew it. You hate lasagna."

"I do not! I just . . . I love lasagna, all right? And be sure to tell that to your mother. I don't want her to think I'm a picky eater."

Leah laughed. "When you're a guest, no one cares if you're picky or not."

"That's what you think," Miguel said darkly. "And anyway, I just don't want to give them an excuse."

"Who?"

"Your parents!"

"An excuse for what?"

Miguel looked at her as if she were being intentionally dense, then away, out the rain-streaked window. "An excuse not to like me," he muttered.

"They're going to love you." Leah didn't let herself think about the things Miguel had already done to offend them, like canceling brunch at the last minute or refusing to meet them at the haunted house. "Just be your usual charming self and you have nothing to worry about."

"Is that some type of crack?" Miguel demanded.

"What are you so worried about?" Leah laughed. "Everything's going to be fine."

"I know," he said grumpily.

"So relax," she advised. "It's only dinner."

"Whatever."

A few weeks before, his attitude would have infuriated her, but she was finally starting to understand him. Down deep, Miguel was shy. It was his fear of the unknown that made him want to control everything. But seeing that he was sweating dinner with her parents beyond any normal parameter, Leah took pity on him and changed the subject yet again.

"I wonder what the city council thought of that story about their budget last night," she said, referring to the TV news. "Peter was great."

Miguel perked up a little. "It'll be *great* if people actually send money." He ate the last bite of his hamburger and wiped his fingers on a crumpled napkin.

"Yeah. Or who knows? Maybe the city council will cough some up, now that they're on the hot seat."

"It would be too bad to lose the bus Peter's friend picked out," he said. "If the council would come up with half, we could probably earn the remaining four thousand pretty fast."

"Probably. I hope that school isn't in a real big hurry to sell it."

Miguel nodded and put down his napkin. "Are you ready to go back?"

She looked out the window and shook her head at the sight of the rain pounding the pavement in sheets. "Are we driving or swimming?"

"Coming here was your bright idea," Miguel reminded her.

They ran for his car, Leah holding her jacket over her hair. Miguel wrestled her door open, then ran around to his, and they both got inside quickly, their wet clothes dripping on the vinyl upholstery. Almost immediately the windows began to fog up. Miguel started the engine and turned the defroster on high.

"This'll look good," Leah teased. "Us showing up at school with steamy windows."

Miguel smiled mischievously and raised his eyebrows. "I'll show you steamy windows," he offered.

"Drive," Leah told him, pointing ahead through the foggy windshield.

Miguel drove, guiding the car carefully along streets that swished with rain. They were only blocks from the high school, and Leah was lost in thought when Miguel snapped her back to the present.

"I went to my old church," he said out of the blue. "I went the night after the haunted house."

"But . . . but it was so *late*," was all she could think of to say.

"Yeah. It was the next morning, actually, if you want to get technical."

"And?" she prompted, guessing there had to be more.

"And I lit a candle for my mother."

Leah smiled crookedly, knowing how much the admission must have cost him. "I'll bet that made her really happy."

Miguel shrugged. "She doesn't know. I don't want to tell her until . . ."

"Until?"

"Until I make up my mind, I guess." He pulled into the crowded CCHS parking lot and started cruising for a space at the edge nearest the buildings. "You know what Peter said? He said you can't be mad at God and not believe in him too."

Leah nodded. "Makes sense."

"Do you believe in God, Leah? I mean, really. Tell me the truth."

"I don't know."

"I don't know either." He sighed. "But I think . . . well . . . I might."

"Ben! Hey, Pipkin!" a voice called out as Ben snuck into the cafeteria with his waterlogged brown bag. Despite the cold, he had intended to eat outside, under the soccer field bleachers, but when the skies had opened up, he'd had to run for cover. "Pipkin! Over here!"

Ben turned to see the guys he had eaten with the week before—Neil, Lance, and Stuart—sitting with five more guys he didn't know. They were all pushed in at one table, waving him over in a way that left no room for argument. It was exactly the type of scene Ben had feared when he'd opted to avoid the cafeteria.

*I should have stayed under the bleachers*, he thought nervously. *Better wet than dead.*

Slowly, his soaked sneakers squishing on the linoleum, Ben walked over to see what they wanted.

"Your program has some type of bug," Stuart said without preamble. "It's totally messing up."

There was immediate agreement from everyone at the table.

"I've locked up like five times," one guy complained.

"At least!" said another.

"So what?" Lance told them. "My mom went to use her appointment book program this morning and it wouldn't even come up. I don't know if it got deleted or corrupted or what. She was fit to be tied, though, and *I* got in trouble." He glared at Ben through narrowed eyes. "What's the deal?"

"I . . . I have no idea." Unfortunately, it wasn't a lie. "My program wouldn't be affecting anything else. Maybe your mom was doing something wrong."

Lance was clearly ready to debate that, but he never got the chance.

"No way!" shouted several people at the table. "It's screwing up my programs, too."

"It can't—" Ben started nervously.

"My computer won't launch my sister's science tutor now, and it can't even find Desert Commandos," said a big guy eating from two full trays.

Ben imagined that the rainwater running off his clothes and pooling at his feet was really a puddle of sweat. There was no way what everyone was describing could be happening. No way. And yet . . . he was pretty sure it was. And that Tomb of Terror had something to do with it.

"Look, there might be some kind of bug on the fourth level," he admitted desperately. "But all that does is lock you up, and I've almost got it worked out anyway." He crossed numb fingers inside his coat pocket. "So anyone who's locking up, just stay below level four. You can still win the game, no problem."

"What about all the other stuff?" Lance demanded. "What about my mom's appointment book?"

"I don't know," Ben said, poised to run if anyone stood up. "Have you scanned for viruses lately?"

"I would, if my virus scan was working," someone else put in sarcastically. "I've got a term paper on that hard drive, Pipkin. If it crashes, you're dead."

The murmurs of agreement around the table made Ben think his murderer would have plenty of help. He played his final card.

"Listen," he told them. "Is my game working or not? I mean, aside from that little glitch on the fourth level, is everyone's machine bringing it up and running it all right?"

He could see them thinking that over. No one said it wasn't working.

"Well, there you go, then," Ben said. "How can

there be something wrong with the game, when the game is running fine?"

He knew his logic was full of holes, but the group at the table seemed to buy it. At least temporarily. He hurried out of the cafeteria while everyone was still mulling that over, tossing his soaked lunch into the trash on the way.

In the gym, his hands shook as he spun out the combination on his locker. He'd managed to get away with most of his newfound dignity intact, but he knew he'd only bought himself a day or two at best. Soon the whole school would be on to him and demanding some sort of fix. If not some sort of retribution . . .

He needed to find out what was wrong with his dad's program. Fast.

"No!" Sandra broke in, shaking her head. "No, I'm sorry. That's not right."

The cheerleaders stopped in the middle of the new dance they were learning and turned to face their coach.

"You have to make those turns on the music, or else it just looks sloppy." Sandra crouched down next to the boom box and rewound the tape to play back the problem section. "Don't you hear that?" she shouted over the music. "Da da da *dum*. Da da da *dum*."

"I'll tell you what's da-da-da-*dumb*," Vanessa

sneered to Tiffany Barrett. The two girls giggled behind their hands.

There was no doubt about it—Vanessa was full of herself that day. Ever since practice had started, she'd been showing off, making jokes, and giving Sandra a hard time. And she'd certainly left no mystery as to the source of her good mood.

"Jesse and I had the most romantic time at the dance!" she'd bragged the second she'd hit the locker room. "He took me to Le Papillon for dinner. Ooh, and I *love* that car! Do you know it's all his?"

Melanie had been tying her shoes at the time, and she'd kept her eyes on her laces. It was so like Vanessa to act as if she were the only girl in the room who had gone to the dance, when in fact all the cheerleaders had.

"He looked so amazing in his tuxedo!" Vanessa had gushed on, pausing to let that sink in. "Didn't you think so, Melanie?"

There had been a hush while the other girls waited for her answer.

"He looked all right," Melanie said grudgingly. "For Jesse."

Vanessa had tittered happily. "I think someone's jealous!" she'd crowed. "Too bad, Melanie! You can't have him back."

"I never wanted him in the first place."

"Maybe that's because you don't know what

you're missing," Vanessa had said with a sly, suggestive smile.

Melanie had grabbed her sweatshirt and left for the gym before Vanessa could get into any disgusting particulars.

"Okay. Now, we're going to do this again, and this time I want everyone to pay attention," Sandra said, rewinding the tape once more. "That means *everyone*, Vanessa."

"What?" Vanessa protested innocently. "Da da da *dum*—I've got it."

"Then how about proving it by turning on the beat this time?"

"I really, *really* like this woman," Tanya whispered to Melanie.

Melanie nodded, but Vanessa was so on her nerves that day that even seeing Sandra bring her down a peg couldn't take the edge off. Melanie knew what Vanessa was thinking—she read it in her smirk every time she looked her way: *I have Jesse and you don't.*

And it wasn't the fact that Vanessa was dating Jesse that Melanie found so annoying. It was the fact that believing she'd taken him from Melanie seemed to give her such a thrill.

The music started up again and the cheerleaders began to dance.

*You have him now*, Melanie thought, casting a dark look Vanessa's way. *Just wait.*

169

# Twelve

"What did you get?" Jenna asked, leaning over Peter's paper.

"What did *you* get?" Peter countered. The two of them had gone straight to Peter's house after school on Wednesday to do homework in his den.

"I asked you first."

"It's your homework." Peter flipped the piece of scratch paper he'd been working on facedown on the coffee table and pinned it with one hand. "I'm only helping."

"It's no help if you don't let me see it." Jenna turned her head away, pretending to sulk. Then, with a swift, sideways grab, she pulled the paper out from under him.

"Ha!" she crowed as she read his answer. "That's what *I* got!"

Peter laughed good-naturedly. "Then either we're right, or we both made the same mistake. My geometry's a little rusty."

"I'm going to assume we're right," Jenna said happily, moving on to the next problem.

Peter returned to the book he was reading for his American novel class. They worked in companionable silence until the telephone rang.

"Peter, it's for you!" Mrs. Altmann called.

Peter rose to pick up the extension in the den. "Hello? . . . Oh. Hi, Reverend Thompson."

Jenna put down her tooth-marked pencil, curious to know why the reverend was calling Peter.

"Really? . . . Really? That's great! . . . Sure, I'll be right over. . . . No, that's okay. Don't worry. . . . All right. I'll see you in a few minutes." He hung up and turned to Jenna with an enormous smile.

"Reverend Thompson said money is pouring in for the bus. People have been stopping by with envelopes for the last couple of days. He was going to give them to us Sunday, but just now the letter carrier brought in a whole boxful of them."

"A boxful?" Jenna gasped, scrambling to her feet.

"Well, he said it was a small box. But still . . . a box! I'm going to go pick it up and bring it back here. Want to come?"

She was already pulling on her raincoat.

"You two be careful in this rain," Peter's mother warned as they walked through the living room to the front door. "Drive slowly."

"We will."

They pulled their hoods up over their heads and dashed through the pelting rain to the car. A few minutes later they pulled into the church parking lot.

Inside the church office, the secretary, Mrs. Stanley, handed them a box a little larger than a shoe box, stuffed full of envelopes. "You got here fast," she remarked. "The reverend just brought this up. He said to tell you he put everything he's received so far in there."

"Wow!" Jenna said, her eyes getting round. "That's a lot of envelopes! How much money do you think there is?"

Mrs. Stanley smiled and shook her head. "I don't know. But the fact that you got so many letters shows people really wish you well. You ought to feel at least as good about that as the money."

"Let's open them now," Jenna said excitedly to Peter. There were a couple of guest chairs and a little end table in the office, and she moved in that direction.

But Peter shook his head. "It'll take too long and make too much of a mess. If we take them back to my house, we can spread out and take our time."

"That might be better," Mrs. Stanley agreed, and Jenna knew she was outvoted.

"All right. But let's hurry. I can't wait to see what we got!"

They thanked Mrs. Stanley, then let themselves out of the office, hesitating under the eaves. The rain was in a lull between cloudbursts, and Jenna was glad they'd be able to get back to the car without getting the envelopes wet. But the next moment she realized she didn't want to go to the car—not right away, anyway.

She turned to Peter. "I wonder if the church is unlocked."

He smiled—his friendly, familiar smile. The smile that said they were definitely best friends. "I was just wondering the same thing."

They trotted across the rain-slick courtyard to the front of the church. The box of envelopes tucked under his left arm, Peter tugged at a front door handle with his right. The heavy door swung open, and he and Jenna slipped inside.

The interior of the church was hushed and dim, the cloudy day outside barely illuminating the stained-glass windows. Jenna breathed in deeply, savoring the usual comforting smell, as the two of them walked a short way down the aisle and slid into a pew near the back. Peter put the box on the worn wood beside him and closed his eyes.

"Dear Lord," he prayed aloud, "thank you for this gift for the Junior Explorers. Sometimes we start thinking we're doing these things on our own, that everything's up to us. So thank you too for this reminder of your daily involvement in our lives. We pray that you'll give us the strength to see this project through and the wisdom to do a good job. In Jesus' name we pray. Amen."

"Amen," Jenna echoed, sniffing back grateful tears. It wasn't just the money, either, that had her all choked up.

*And Lord,* she added silently, *thank you for my friend, Peter, and for bringing us back together. I don't know what I would do without him!*

"I'll get it!" Nicole sang out, wondering who would be ringing their doorbell so close to dinnertime. She put down the handful of silverware she'd been setting the table with and ran to find out.

"Jesse!" she gasped. "What are you doing here?"

"Hey, Nicole." His smile was uncertain—especially for him. "Is this a bad time?"

"No. Well, we're about to eat dinner."

"I was afraid of that. I'll just see you at school tomorrow." He turned and started to leave.

"No, wait!" she cried, stepping out onto the porch and closing the door behind her. "I've still got a few minutes. What's up?"

He shrugged. "I don't know. I thought maybe you'd want to get a pizza or something. But it was just a last-minute idea. I should have called. . . ."

"No!" she said excitedly. "Pizza sounds great."

"But you're already about to eat."

"It's just tuna casserole. My mom won't mind. Wait here." She left him on the doorstep and hurried inside to find her mother taking the casserole out of the oven.

"Mom, can I go have pizza with Jesse?" Nicole asked hurriedly. "Please?"

"What? We're about to eat dinner."

"I know. But it's *Jesse*, Mom. I'll do all the dishes when I get home. Just leave everything on the table and I'll take care of it. Okay? *Please?*"

Mrs. Brewster sighed as she set the heavy casserole on a trivet. "I'm going to hold you to that, Nicole."

"Thanks! Oh, thanks!" She hugged her mom hurriedly and ran for the door, pausing only long enough to grab a coat from the hall closet and check her hair in the mirror.

"Hey, where are you going?" Heather demanded, coming down the stairs just then.

"A magical place called None of Your Business," Nicole told her, feeling very witty. Before Heather could make a scene, she was out the door.

Jesse was waiting in the car, the engine already running, and Nicole rushed to join him. "Where are we going?" she asked as she let herself in and buckled her seat belt.

Jesse shrugged. "Is there any good pizza in this town? Because if there is, I haven't found it."

"Slice of Rome, downtown. They're real good."

"All right."

Jesse backed out of the driveway and turned the car toward downtown. Nicole gave him directions to the restaurant, then racked her brain for a conversation starter. All she could come up with was Eight Prime or football. They *always* talked about Eight Prime and football. And even though the "away" game against the Lakeview Hurricanes was only two nights off, she desperately wanted some other topic.

Jesse finally broke the silence. "I, uh, I guess you're probably wondering what this is all about."

"I thought it was about pizza."

"Yeah, but you're not surprised to see me?"

"It's getting to the point where nothing you do surprises me, Jesse. Even trying to guess wears me out." Until it was out of her mouth, Nicole had no idea she was going to say that. She hadn't even known she thought it. But it was true, she realized. She shrank down in her seat a little, wondering if he'd be mad.

On the contrary, Jesse seemed amused. "That's probably the first honest thing you've ever said to me," he replied with a chuckle.

She thought about that the rest of the way to the pizzeria.

They were there early that Wednesday, so Slice of Rome was all but empty. The waitress gave them a choice corner booth.

"We'll have a large Hawaiian," Jesse told the woman, waving away the menus she offered. "And a couple of salads, and a pitcher of Coke."

"Yuck!" Nicole objected. "Not pineapple. Not on a pizza."

Jesse looked surprised to be contradicted, but after a moment he sighed. "I keep forgetting I'm living in the sticks. All right, make half of it whatever she wants," he told the waitress.

"Pepperoni and mushroom," Nicole said quickly, "and house dressing for the salads—on the side. And make that pitcher *Diet* Coke."

"Okay, that's where I draw the line. Just bring us two separate drinks and cancel the pitcher, all right?"

The waitress walked off scratching out half the stuff on her pad.

"So what's up with you tonight?" Jesse asked. "Are you taking this new honesty thing to extremes, or what?"

"What do you mean?"

"I mean that last week you would have eaten whatever I ordered and sworn it was your favorite."

*He's right,* she realized, not liking the way that knowledge made her feel. *But that was before. . . .*

"Jesse, why are we here?" she asked suddenly. "I mean, am I just your fallback plan when Melanie can't make it, and Vanessa can't make it, and you don't have anything else to do?"

"Ugh! Vanessa," he groaned, squeezing his eyes shut as if the mere word gave him a headache. "What a mistake that was!"

"What do you mean?"

"I just asked her to a dance—one dance. Then it

turned into the bonfire and the dance, but that was all it was supposed to be. By the time I dropped her off, though, I think she was wording the wedding invitations. You have no idea how much I wish I'd taken you instead."

"Really?" Nicole's heart leapt at the unexpected admission.

"Yeah, but I had a good reason not to. I didn't know Vanessa would make that dance into more than it was. But I was certain you would. And I just don't like you that way, Nicole."

"Thanks. I remember," she muttered sullenly, her hopes dashed again.

"No, it's because I didn't want to hurt you! I mean, I was kind of hoping . . . the reason I wanted to see you tonight . . . I like you, Nicole. As a friend, I mean. You're the only one who stuck by me, really, through all those problems at school."

"That's because I like you too, Jes—"

"No, don't say it like that." He hesitated. "I still feel bad about what happened at Hank Lundgreen's party."

"Why are you telling me this?" she asked, wincing at the painful remembrance of the kisses they'd shared that night.

"Because I'm hoping maybe we can be friends. *Actual* friends, not whatever we are now. There's never going to be anything romantic between us. But if you stop flirting with me, I'll stop toying with you, and maybe we can have some sort of nice, normal friendship. What do you say?"

"I do *not* flirt with you!" Nicole protested.

Jesse laughed. "Oops. So much for honesty."

Nicole could feel herself blushing. "Well, okay. Maybe I do, a little. But can I help it if I think we'd be great together?"

"It isn't going to happen, Nicole," he said gently. "And I'm not saying that to be mean, or because I think I'm too good, or anything else. We're just two different people."

Nicole nodded, the beginnings of tears brimming in her eyes.

"You know, when I drove you home after practice the other day, you really made me laugh—all that stuff about Kilriley eating bugs. I've been thinking about that a lot since then."

"You have?"

He smiled. "Yeah. I have. And I'd like to be able to drive you home more often—or ask you to go for a pizza, or even take you to a formal if neither of us has a date—without worrying you'll get the wrong idea."

He paused, then shrugged. "I guess I've never really been friends with a girl before. And don't get me wrong," he hurried to add. "I'm not saying we'll be *best* friends. This isn't going to be some Peter-and-Jenna thing. But just friends. Do you think you could handle that?"

The weird thing was, she was starting to think she could. What she couldn't handle anymore was the burden of such a thoroughly hopeless crush. In a way, Jesse was offering her back her freedom. His friendship and the chance to walk away with some dignity were more like bonus prizes.

Nicole took a deep, shaky breath, then made up her mind.

"I can handle it," she said.

The moment dinner was over, Ben jumped up from the table, intent on getting back to his computer.

"Where are you going, Benny?" his mother asked, heaving herself out of the chair nearest the kitchen. "What are you in such a hurry for?"

"Homework," Ben said, running for the stairs. He repeated it all the way up. "Homework, homework, homework."

It wasn't a lie. Not exactly. He'd never studied harder in his life than he had in the last two days. And if cutting-edge 3D computer graphics weren't part of the CCHS curriculum, that only made his argument for calling them *home*work that much stronger. All afternoon he'd been trying to find the bug he'd somehow programmed into his father's game, with no success. Less than no success, actually, because the more he tried, the more defective his computer got.

He reached his room, shut the door tight, and dropped into the rolling chair in front of his computer. He had switched the power off for dinner because leaving it on was an irrational pet peeve of his mother's—and the last thing he needed at this point was to attract unwelcome attention. He flipped it on now, impatient for the machine to come up.

But it didn't. It announced its BIOS, checked its memory, then froze.

"Uh-oh," Ben said, feeling slightly queasy as he punched the Reset button. "This is bad. Really, really bad."

When his computer froze again in the exact same place, the tears he'd been holding back all week finally started down his cheeks. The way his programs had been deteriorating, he was pretty sure his hard drive was toast. And if it was, he didn't even want to think about what was happening to students' hard drives all over Clearwater Crossing.

*You have to tell Dad*, he thought. He hit the Reset button again. No improvement. He thought he might be able to get going again with a boot disk, but then what? *You have to tell him.*

He took several long, deep breaths, wiped his face, and blew his nose. Then he went to find his father. Ironically, Mr. Pipkin was hard at work on A-Mazed as well.

"Hey, Ben!" he said excitedly as Ben walked into the den. "I've just finished fixing those little things I was telling you about in A-Mazed. I've been working on it at lunch this week, because I know you're eager to give it to friends. I'll check it for bugs tonight, and then the game's all yours. Look at this mummy go now. It's really cool."

Ben took a long, miserable look at the half-unwrapped mummy tearing maniacally around his father's computer screen. "It *is* cool," he said finally. "I wish I hadn't deleted it."

"What are you talking about?" His dad was still absorbed by the image. "You can't delete it."

"You can if you go into the code."

Mr. Pipkin finally looked up. "Why would someone do that?"

"I took a version of A-Mazed to my room," Ben admitted. "I wanted to fix it so I could give it to people, but the mummy wouldn't work no matter what I did. In the end, I just took it out of the code."

"You did? You got the mummy completely out?"

Ben nodded unhappily.

"But that's *good*, Ben!" his father exclaimed.

"It is?"

"Sure! I mean, you should have asked me for a copy, but you didn't hurt the master, so it doesn't matter. In the meantime, I didn't realize you'd learned so much code. You're turning into quite a programmer."

Ben put one hand to his aching head and pushed his limp hair back. "Well, that's actually what I wanted to talk to you about."

And quickly, before his mother could come out of the kitchen, Ben spilled the whole pathetic story. He told his father how he had modified the game and posted it on the school Web site. He told him about the problems everyone was having with their other programs now. And, last but not least, he told him about the current sad state of his computer upstairs. "I think I fried the hard drive somehow," he concluded. "And if it happened to mine—"

"You put A-Mazed on the Internet?" his father said in angry disbelief. "You told me you wanted to give it to a few friends!"

"Well, yeah. A few friends at school."

"*Hundreds* of people could have that game now. You have no way of knowing."

"No, I'm pretty sure I know, because they're all telling me," Ben replied unhappily. "Dad, I'm really sorry. I never should have done it. But if you don't help me, I'm dead. I've tried and tried, and I can't figure out how I messed up. And now my computer's down, so I'm pretty sure others are down, or *about* to go down. If I go to school tomorrow without an answer—"

"But I still don't understand *why*, Ben," Mr. Pipkin said. "Why did you give out that program after I specifically told you not to?"

Ben squirmed, hating having to admit his own inadequacy. "I just . . . wanted people to like me," he confessed, hanging his head. "I wanted to fit in."

There was a long silence. Then finally a noise from his father made Ben look up in amazement. Mr. Pipkin was laughing!

"Boy, do I know how that feels," he acknowledged. "I was practically the biggest dork in school. But you're not like me, Ben. You're much more with it than I was! And you have lots of friends."

Ben shook his head. "Not really."

"What about Eight Prime?"

"They don't like me. They put up with me, but they don't . . . I thought if everyone at school believed I'd designed a great computer game, though—"

"Wait a minute," his father interrupted. "You told them *you* designed A-Mazed?"

*Oops.* "Well, actually, it's called Tomb of Terror now."

"Tomb of Terror!" Mr. Pipkin whooped. He was starting to find the situation pretty amusing. "You don't think that's a little much?"

"Probably. Dad, please, *please*, could you look at my computer?"

"Oh, definitely. You couldn't keep me away now."

The two of them went up to Ben's room, where his father took the desk chair while Ben hovered worriedly behind him. Mr. Pipkin used a boot disk to get the machine up and running, then started looking through the code Ben had altered.

"You know, I tried to make myself popular in high school once," he said as he worked. "What a disaster that was!" He shook his head and chuckled to himself, remembering. "At least *you* tried to do something smart. I went out and spent all my money on this white suit, like John Travolta's in *Saturday Night Fever*, and I actually wore it to school—Mr. Disco King himself! What a nightmare. People teased me about it for a year afterward. Be glad you were smarter than that, at least."

"Uh, I guess," Ben said, with a clandestine sideways glance at the storage box under his bed. It was official. He and his father *were* clones.

"You know, the thing is, now I wouldn't change who I am for anything. I'm happy now, Ben— happier than I've ever been in my life. I have you and your mother. I have a job I love. Every day I wake up thankful for the brain I have and for what it lets me do."

"That's because you're old, Dad," Ben ventured. "No one cares about being popular after they're old."

Mr. Pipkin laughed. "You'd be surprised how

popular I am. Every time someone at work has a computer problem they can't solve, they come running straight to me."

"That's not the same thing."

"No. But maybe it's not as different as you think. Being popular is its own kind of job. And if it's the job you think you want, then it doesn't hurt to apply for it. But ultimately, at the end of the day, it's a lot more worthwhile to recognize and hang on to the friends you already have than to wear yourself out pleasing strangers."

"I guess," Ben grumbled, more interested in the code his father was skimming through than in what the man was saying.

"When you get a little older, you'll *know*. A few true friends beat a bunch of fickle acquaintances every time."

Mr. Pipkin stopped scrolling and opened another file. "Oops."

"Oops what?" Ben asked nervously, leaning forward.

"Go ask your mom to make a pot of coffee, all right? This is going to take a while."

# Thirteen

"Here. Take one of these patch disks and an instruction sheet," Ben said, passing out disks and flyers to the angry mob gathered around him in the hall Thursday morning. "I'm really sorry, but this will fix everything."

People pushed and jostled each other to get the repair program, most of them giving Ben dirty looks as they snatched the materials from his hands.

"Don't worry, I have lots," he told them, "and it's posted on the school Web site."

Tomb of Terror, on the other hand, was no longer available that way. Mr. Pipkin had hacked into the site and removed it the night before, in addition to posting the fix for anyone off campus who might need it.

As it had turned out, Ben had made two mistakes in his programming. The lockup on the fourth level was merely an inconvenience, the result of inadvertently deleting some necessary code along with the mummy. The big mistake had turned out to be the code he'd mistakenly put into the computer system registry instead of the high score file. Every time a computer was turned on after Tomb of Terror had been loaded, the stray code overwrote needed information, gradually crippling the system.

He and his father had stayed up nearly all night designing a comprehensive patch program to uninstall Tomb of Terror and repair the damage it had done. Mr. Pipkin had dubbed it Patch of Panic. And while Ben didn't necessarily appreciate his father's sense of humor, by the wee hours of that morning, he had come to appreciate his father as never before. How many dads would lose nearly a whole night's sleep bailing their son out of such a stupid mistake and be so nice about it too?

"Hey, Pipkin!" a harsh new voice shouted at the back of the crowd. "I have a late paper because of you!"

"I know. I'm sorry," Ben mumbled tiredly. "Just take one of these and follow the instructions. I promise it will fix everything."

The first bell of the day finally rang, and the crowd surged anxiously toward him. "Don't worry! I have lots," Ben repeated. "I'll be handing them out in the cafeteria at lunchtime."

A few last anxious people snatched disks from his hands, but eventually the mob drifted off to class. Ben was finally able to open his locker.

"Hi, Ben," a girl's voice said behind him as he rooted for his books.

"Take a disk and an instruction sheet," he mumbled, passing them over his shoulder without turning around. "This will fix everything."

"No, Ben, it's me!" Jenna laughed. "I heard what happened with your computer game. I guess you're having a pretty bad morning, huh?"

Ben's eyes were so tired and bloodshot he felt as if he were blinking over sand. He'd had to wear his glasses instead of contacts, and even so Jenna's smile seemed slightly out of focus. "I'm glad you think it's so funny," he said sarcastically, "since you're the one who caused it all."

"*Me?* What did I do?"

Ben was too exhausted to play games. "You lied to me about going to the dance with Peter. You could have just said you didn't want to go with me."

"Ben! No, I—"

"Even nerds have feelings, Jenna. I thought if *you* were desperate enough to lie to me, then anybody would have. So I decided to change my image. I bought those stupid clothes, then I stole my father's computer program—"

"I didn't lie to you, Ben!" Jenna said, distressed. "I had no idea . . . I really thought I *was* going with Peter."

"Did you think the *two* of you were going out with Melanie?"

"I didn't find out about Peter taking Melanie until the next day. And when I did, I was so upset . . . well, I didn't want to go at all. I wish I had realized . . . I would have explained. I just figured it was obvious that something had gone wrong between me and Peter. I never guessed you'd think I'd *lied* to you, though. I thought we were friends!"

"We are." Ben was starting to feel a little foolish about jumping to conclusions.

"Well, don't friends trust each other?"

"I guess." The bell went off. They were both late to class. "Listen, Jenna, I'm so tired right now, I really don't know what I'm saying. I just . . . I'm sorry, all right? I don't know how I could have thought you'd lie to me either. I just started thinking that no one in Eight Prime liked me and—"

"Ben! We do too! Who made up the name Eight Prime in the first place?"

"I did."

"So what happened to 'one number, indivisible, with liberty and justice for all'?"

"I don't know. I must have gotten amnesia or something."

Jenna smiled and touched his arm. "Eat lunch with me and Peter today. We'll do our best to fill you in."

"Right," he said before she hurried off to class. As he watched her go, he wondered if he'd ever felt more like a dope. Then he smiled.

For a dope, he felt pretty good.

———

"Boy, wait till you hear what happened," Peter told Melanie Thursday night. "Do I have a big announcement!"

"Well, come on in and tell us," she said, ushering him and Jenna into the Andrewses' poolhouse. "Everyone's here."

Melanie had left the outdoor landscape lights on and the gate to the backyard open so that her friends could bypass the house and come directly to the poolhouse. Everyone was gathered in the main room, parked on the Hawaiian-print furniture that dominated the glassed-in space. Melanie had closed the blinds for privacy and set up snacks on the large built-in bar at the end of the room, making the poolhouse feel like a comfy secret clubhouse.

Peter and Jenna walked over to join the group, and Peter set a cardboard box on the low glass table in the center. "Those are the letters that have come into our church since I was on the news," he said, smiling broadly.

"What? No way!" Nicole exclaimed. She pushed out of her chair, dropping to her knees beside the table to riffle through the envelopes.

"Peter! That's a lot!" said Melanie.

Peter beamed as he sat sideways on a large, upholstered chaise. Jenna sat beside him, her smile as big as his.

"I know!" he said. "People are really behind us. Not all of those letters included money, but they

191

were all really encouraging. And a lot of them *did* have money."

"Two thousand, four hundred and eight dollars and forty-two cents," Jenna said proudly. "That's everything up through today's mail."

"Two thousand dollars!" Nicole gasped, impressed.

"Forty-two cents?" Leah queried with raised eyebrows.

"Little kids sent change," Peter explained. "They raided their piggy banks to help the Junior Explorers."

"That's so sweet!" Melanie cried.

"Forget about sweet—that's a lot of money!" Jesse said. "And money for nothing, too."

"So how much do we have now?" Miguel asked from his seat beside Leah.

"Eight thousand, one hundred sixty-four dollars and twenty-five cents," Ben replied promptly. Everyone turned to stare at him with open mouths. "What?" he said defensively. "I'm good with numbers."

"I'll say," Peter agreed. "That's exactly right."

"Listen to this," Nicole broke in, reading a letter from the box. " 'Dear Eight Prime: Those kids should get a bus. The city guys should walk. Yours truly, Ryan Smith. P.S. I had more money, but my sister spent it on candy.' "

Everyone laughed as Nicole held up the blue-lined sheet of notebook paper to show the rows of cut tape that had held Ryan's coins.

"There were a few like that," Jenna said. "It makes you feel so good to read them—to know that even little kids understand and want to help."

"I feel kind of bad about taking their piggy bank money, though," Melanie said.

"I don't." Peter shook his head. "They want to help, and I think we should respect that and thank them, the same way we would an adult."

"I'll bet their parents are really proud," Jenna added.

She and Peter smiled at each other—again—and Peter bent to whisper in her ear. Jenna nodded happily.

Melanie felt something stir in the pit of her stomach. Whatever the disagreement between those two had been, they'd obviously patched it up. They seemed as close now as they'd been the very first day she'd met them, at the volunteer meeting for Kurt Englbehrt's carnival.

*You should be happy for them*, she thought. And she was. Just not as happy as she wanted to be. Seeing the two of them together made Melanie's big night alone with Peter seem impossibly far in the past. And there was something that told her, some sixth sense, that there wouldn't be another.

Not that they hadn't had fun. They'd had a great time. But when Peter had said good-night, he hadn't tried to kiss her. And she hadn't tried to change his mind. Now, watching him from across the room, Melanie thought she was beginning to understand why.

Peter found contentment everywhere—in his friends, his church, the Junior Explorers. Maybe she didn't like him so much as she wanted to *be* like him. She liked him—she liked him a lot. But maybe romance was off the track.

"So what's the word on the bus?" Leah asked Peter, crashing into Melanie's thoughts. "Have they sold it to someone else yet?"

"No, not yet," he replied. "But I don't know how long they'll wait."

"Do you think people will keep sending money?" Nicole asked, still pawing through the box.

"I wouldn't be surprised if we got a little more. But there were a lot fewer letters today than yesterday. I think it's tapering off."

"So that means more fund-raisers," Miguel said matter-of-factly.

Melanie liked the way he said it, as if he didn't mind. She smiled at him and Leah.

"Hey, I have an idea," Jesse piped up. "Maybe Ben here could write a program that erases everyone's computers, and this time we'll *sell* the patch disks."

"Very funny," Ben sniffed. His new contacts made his eyes seem even browner and more puppy-like than before.

"I don't think it's funny at all," Jenna said disapprovingly.

"Me either," Leah agreed.

Jesse looked at Nicole, obviously expecting her to rush to his rescue, but Nicole only shrugged. "Sorry. Me either."

"Geez!" he exclaimed. "I was kidding! Can't you people take a joke?"

"You wouldn't think it was so funny if it happened to you," Ben muttered. "You have no idea what I've been through."

"No, of course not," Jesse said sarcastically. "*I've* never stepped in it at school. Getting kicked off the team was tons of fun."

Everyone stared at him, amazed he'd raised that touchy subject himself. And then they started to laugh. All of them—even Jesse.

"He's got you there, Ben," Melanie chuckled. "But is it really so bad at school? I mean, it was an honest mistake. Don't people understand?"

"People get really crabby when you disable their computers. And the less they know about them, the more they panic. This afternoon, a guy actually threatened to kill me if I'd lost his history paper. I mean, everyone's been saying stuff like that, but this guy really meant it. I said I was sorry—I admitted I messed up—but the genius didn't even have a backup."

"The next time someone threatens to hurt you, you send them to me," Miguel said, his dark eyes intense. "That's not acceptable."

"Well—I—" Ben sputtered, obviously surprised by Miguel's offer.

"It's better to avoid people like that if you can," Peter said. "Why don't you hang out with us for a while, until this all blows over? You know where Jenna and I eat lunch."

"Yeah, or you'd be welcome to eat with us," Melanie offered.

"At the *cheerleaders'* table?" Ben gasped, his eyes enormous.

"Ben's right. Be serious, Melanie," said Jesse. "He can't sit with a bunch of girls. You can squeeze in at my table, bud. No one will so much as look at you there."

"Yeah? Well, thanks, you guys. Thanks a lot," Ben muttered, staring at the floor. His voice was unsteady, as if he might cry. "I, uh . . . I need to use the bathroom."

"It's back there." Melanie pointed over her shoulder. She almost added that there was Kleenex in the cupboard, but she didn't want to embarrass him. She thought it was kind of sweet how Ben had choked up at the way the group had rallied around him—she could have used a tissue herself.

"So what's the next fund-raiser?" she asked to cover the awkward gap when he'd gone.

"Oh! Peter's got an idea," Jenna said excitedly.

"How about a pancake breakfast?" Peter proposed. "Reverend Thompson said we could have it at the church and use the kitchen and main hall. We wouldn't have to rent anything, because the church already owns everything. And we'd get a ton of help, too. Our congregation has breakfast down to a science."

Leah laughed. "Team Take-out strikes again!"

"Fine with me, I guess," said Jesse. "Flipping pancakes has got to be easier than flipping burgers."

"How so?" Nicole demanded.

"Because you don't end up covered in grease, for one thing. I smelled like meat musk for a solid week after that carnival. It was oozing out of my pores."

"Gross!" Nicole squealed.

Miguel laughed. "Mine too."

"We'll still have some type of meat, though, right?" Melanie asked. "I mean, at every pancake breakfast I've ever been to, they served ham or sausage or something."

"Good point," said Leah. "What would we have on our menu?"

"Does that mean we're going to do it?" Peter asked.

Everyone nodded.

"Melanie, is it okay with you?"

"Sure." She knew he asked because it was going to be held at his church, but she was actually glad of an excuse to finally see it—even if she'd only be in the kitchen.

"What did I miss? What did I miss?" Ben asked, walking back in and grabbing twin handfuls of chips on his way past the bar. Two steps later, they began raining down on the indoor-outdoor carpeting. "Oops. Sorry, Melanie."

She waved away his apology. "No problem. We're talking about having a pancake breakfast at Peter's church. How's that sound?"

"Cool! Hey, can we get chefs' hats this time? You know, those tall, puffy white ones? Those are really neat."

"Yeah. Neat," said Nicole, shaking her head. "Or maybe we can all just wear hair nets."

Ben looked at her as if she were crazy. "Hair nets aren't cool. Get a grip, Nicole!"

# Fourteen

Ben lurked in a side stairwell, steeling himself to face the early-morning crowd in the main hallway. His stomach was full of butterflies and his backpack was full of patch disks. And while he didn't expect to see too many people still in need of repair, he wasn't taking any chances. After all, it *was* Friday the thirteenth.

With one last deep breath, he stepped out into the hallway, holding his head high. If nothing else, he knew Eight Prime was behind him now. He had offers of protection and lunchtime company. He'd enjoyed a few brief days of glory. In short, he was no worse off than he'd started out.

A couple of people accosted him as he made his way to his locker. Ben gave them patch disks and instructions, along with his apologies. At least they seemed calmer than the group the day before had. Hopefully word was getting out that the patch worked fine.

Then, a little farther down the hall, a kid he'd

seen before came running up. "Hi, Ben," he called. "Remember me?"

Ben remembered him all too well. It was the guy who'd first told him about the problem with the secret door.

"Sure. Mark, right?" Ben said, reaching into his pack for another disk.

"Yeah, right. Oh, I don't need a patch," Mark said quickly when he saw what Ben was holding. "I got the repair off the Web last night. That's a slick program, by the way. It's amazing how it fixes everything with only a few keystrokes."

"Thanks," Ben said dubiously. He certainly hadn't expected to hear any compliments on the patch. "We tried to make it as easy as possible."

"We?"

"Me and my dad. Mostly my dad."

"Your dad's into computers too? Man, my dad doesn't know a hard disk from a CD-ROM."

"Actually," Ben admitted, "my dad's a professional programmer. Tomb of Terror was really his game. Except for the bugs, of course—I'm afraid those were all mine."

Mark seemed taken aback. "But when you posted it, you said it was designed by—"

"Benjamin Pipkin. I know. We have the same name. I did want people to think it was mine, though. That's why I added my picture."

Mark looked disappointed, but then he smiled.

"I guess I can understand that. Aside from that glitch on the fourth level, that's one of the coolest games I've ever played."

"Yeah? Well that secret door was never a problem in my dad's version, plus he's got a mummy on that level now, chasing everyone around. It's twice as cool as before."

"Where did your dad learn to design computer games?"

Ben shrugged. "It's just something he picked up for fun. He works at ComAm. Do you know who they are?"

"Do I! Man, you are so lucky!" Mark exclaimed. "I wish my dad was cool like yours."

"My dad?"

As if by reflex, Ben's brain conjured up the glasses, the pocket protector, the socks that didn't match. But for the very first time, those things seemed unimportant. What was a lack of fashion sense weighed against his father's intelligence, or kindness, or generosity? Ben felt his heart swell with pride in his father, with respect . . . maybe even with honor.

"Yeah. My dad *is* pretty cool," he said slowly.

The first bell rang.

"I don't want to be late for homeroom," Mark said in a rush. "There's a guy in the front who trips me whenever I have to walk past him. He's such a jerk."

"I know the type."

"Hey, would you want to meet me at lunchtime? I mean, if you're not already busy with a bunch of other people."

"Well, a few of my friends did invite me. . . ."

Mark's face fell. "Yeah, I get it. Well, maybe I'll see you around sometime, then." He started off down the hall.

"No, wait!" Ben called after him. Mark turned around.

"Meet me by the lunch line. My friends will understand."

"Great lasagna, Mrs. Rosenthal," Miguel said, putting down his fork.

"I'm glad you liked it, Miguel." But there was a trace of skepticism in her mother's voice, and Leah knew what she was thinking: He hadn't eaten very much.

"Um, yes," he said awkwardly. "It was very good."

It had been that way all through dinner. Leah could tell Miguel was trying to be polite, but he was coming off so stiff, so wary. It made her normally cordial parents wary too. Making conversation during dinner had proved to be such uphill work that there had been several lengthy periods where nothing had been heard at all but the self-conscious clicking of silverware. Leah had gradually realized she'd completely forgotten how reserved Miguel could be.

It was actually a relief when her parents had given up asking him questions and started talking between themselves about things at Clearwater University, where they were both professors. Now that dinner was over, though, the way was clear for another awkward attempt at conversation. Surprisingly, it was Miguel who made the effort.

"So how about Leah winning that U.S. Girls thing?" he asked her parents. "You must be pretty proud."

Leah would have preferred another topic, but at least he was talking.

"Well . . . we have mixed feelings, just like Leah," Mrs. Rosenthal answered honestly. "We don't really see our daughter as a model, but the scholarship angle is very appealing."

"If she wins the finals, there'll be a lot more in it for her than the scholarship," said Miguel. "People will see her. People will know who she is. It could open a lot of doors."

Leah tossed her head. "You're obsessed with this thing, I swear," she teased. "You probably wish there was a U.S. Boys contest."

Miguel answered her jest seriously. "Not unless they're paying cash. What would I do with a scholarship?"

"Go to college?" Mr. Rosenthal suggested ironically. "That's what's usually done with them."

Miguel shook his head. "I don't have time for that. I have to get a job."

An abrupt, shocked silence descended upon the table. Even Leah couldn't believe what she'd just heard.

"You can go to college and still work part-time," Mrs. Rosenthal ventured. "A lot of students do."

"Yeah. They work unskilled, minimum-wage jobs that maybe pay for their books," said Miguel. "I need a real job—a career."

"Like what?" Leah's father asked. "What kind of career?"

Miguel shrugged. "I've worked construction the last two summers for an old friend of my father's."

"You want to make a career as a construction worker," Leah's mother said. Her tone was pleasant, but there was an undercurrent to it that made Leah wince.

"No. I want to be a contractor. A contractor is in charge. A contractor is his own boss." Miguel shrugged. "But you have to start somewhere."

"But Miguel," Leah protested. "If you want to build things, why not study architecture? Or engineering?"

He looked at her as if she'd just stabbed him in the back. "I need the money, Leah." His eyes warned her not to pursue it.

"But that's what need-based scholarships are for!" she blurted out anyway. "Just because you don't have the money doesn't mean you can't go to college."

"That's a handout. And I don't want it." Miguel's expression had turned angry, defensive.

Leah glanced from him to her parents. Both of them were staring at her, their raised eyebrows speaking louder than words. She dropped her gaze to the shreds of leftover pasta on her plate, knowing it would be a long, long time before she could eat lasagna without remembering this moment.

The silence stretched out, every second more uncomfortable. Leah knew she ought to say something, but she didn't know what. She supposed she ought to defend Miguel's decision, but she didn't know how. The truth was, she agreed with her parents.

*Maybe if we talk about it, I can change his mind,* she thought, glancing up.

But one peek at his stormy face and she looked nervously back at her plate.

"Dessert?" Mrs. Rosenthal asked finally.

Jesse stood by himself on the sidelines, a few yards away from the crowded bench. On the field, the Wildcats were being pounded by the Lakeview Hurricanes. With their undefeated season so far, CCHS could lose the game and still advance to the play-offs. But Jesse didn't want to lose the game—not his first game back.

*Why doesn't Coach put me in?* he thought over and over again. *He said he'd let me play.*

Eric Spenser was doing all right in Jesse's old position, but Jesse knew he could do better. He'd been playing well in practice again. And he was an original starter. He had a feeling he'd rip up the field, if only Coach would give him a chance.

"Jones! Get out there and give Spenser a rest!" Coach Davis finally bellowed.

Jesse streaked out onto the grass. Spenser had been tackled so often that his uniform was thick with mud, and he seemed happy to be replaced. He nodded almost gratefully before he trotted off the field.

Adrenaline flooded Jesse's veins. Here was his chance to show everyone what he could do. The team was down—if he could pull a victory out of this somehow, he'd be a hero again!

And for a while, it seemed as if that was exactly what would happen. The Wildcats were behind by two touchdowns and a field goal when Jesse finally got into the game. But on only his second play, he ran in a pass for a Wildcats touchdown. Switching to defense, he covered his man like a second skin, and when the Wildcats got the ball again, he rushed for most of the yards that ended in his team's next score. The guys were looking at him with some respect again. Hank was even calling plays around him. It seemed the Wildcats were going to pull it off. . . .

But in the end, they were defeated by the clock. Time ran out, with CCHS still down by three points.

"Great effort, Jones," Coach Davis rasped as Jesse climbed onto the team bus for the long, silent ride back to Clearwater Crossing. "You gave it your best shot."

"Yeah."

*But who cares?* Jesse thought, flinging himself into an empty seat at the back. *If I hadn't gotten into trouble, I'd have started. And if I'd started, we'd have won.*

How long was one stupid mistake going to ruin his whole life?

# Fifteen

"Bye-bye, Amy," Jenna called to the little girl running out of the activities center.

"Bye," Amy tossed back over her shoulder.

Amy was the last Junior Explorer to be picked up from the park that Saturday, and Jenna watched at the windows as the first-grader threw herself into her father's arms. Mr. Robbins waved through the glass to Jenna, but Amy took off without a backward glance.

"I don't think Amy likes me as much as she does Melanie," Jenna told Peter with a sigh.

He laughed. "Don't feel bad—I don't think she likes me that much, either. Those two have really bonded."

"Maybe because they've both lost their mothers. That has to be so hard, especially for a girl."

Chris Hobart and his girlfriend, Maura Kennedy, walked over to join them. "We have to get going," Chris, Peter's partner in the Junior Explorers, said. "Maura's supposed to be at her aunt's house in a few minutes. Do you need help picking up these mats, or . . . ?"

"We can get them," said Peter. "You guys go on."

"Bye, then," Maura said. "See you guys later."

Jenna watched as they headed off together, hand in hand.

*It's just like old times again*, she realized happily. *Me helping Peter with the Junior Explorers. Chris and Maura here instead of Eight Prime.*

Not that she didn't like Eight Prime, but she'd missed these times together with Peter. It felt good to be back in their old pattern.

"Well, what do you say? Should we get started on these mats?" Peter asked.

It had rained that morning, so the Junior Explorers had played inside the activities center. A couple dozen folding mats had been dragged out of the storage closet and placed side by side on the floor, creating a large, padded area for the kids to turn cartwheels and somersaults on.

"I'll bring them over, and you stack them," Jenna proposed.

"Good enough."

The two of them got to work, Jenna dragging the mats over one or two at a time. They weren't very big, but they were still pretty heavy. Peter collapsed them along their creases into more manageable rectangles, then stacked them neatly in the closet.

"Oops, sorry," he said, accidentally brushing into her as he reached backward for a mat.

"That's okay."

Space was tight around the closet. When she brought him the next one, she bumped into him. It was unavoidable. More bumping and brushing occurred as more mats were retrieved and stacked. It seemed there was no way to miss each other, short of her leaving the mats in the middle of the room. They nearly knocked heads on the next one. Peter laughed at their clumsiness.

And suddenly Jenna's heart was racing like crazy. It was so silly, so immature . . . but the air seemed full of electricity. She wondered if Peter felt it too, or if it was all in her mind.

*It must be*, she thought. *You're imagining things*.

All the same, when she brought the next mat to the closet, she pulled it in close enough to sneak a look at his face. They were shoulder to shoulder, practically cheek to cheek. She turned her head slightly to peek at his expression. He turned his at the same time. Their gazes locked. Their faces were only inches apart. . . .

And then Peter leaned forward and kissed her— the lightest, briefest kiss. A brush of his lips against hers. She stared at him disbelievingly, barely even sure it had happened.

Peter blushed and looked away. "I'm sorry. I've been wanting to do that for months," he confessed in a low, embarrassed voice. "But it won't ever happen again. Not if you don't want it to."

Jenna's emotions were so wild and confused, she didn't even know what to say.

Then, suddenly, she did. Slipping her arms around Peter, she pressed her cheek against his.

"I want it to," she whispered.


"Stay calm. You can do this," Leah reassured herself. But as she knocked at Miguel's front door, she was still trying to figure out what she'd say when she saw him.

There was no denying that dinner with her parents the night before had been a complete disaster. Still, there had to be some way to smooth things over. At the very least, she wanted to make sure he wasn't mad.

Miguel answered the door himself.

"Hi," Leah said tentatively.

He shrugged.

"Can I come in?"

"I guess."

They sat on the living room sofa. Leah could hear Rosa and Mrs. del Rios talking in the kitchen, busy with some sort of project, so she kept her voice low, hoping to keep Miguel to herself long enough to explain.

"Miguel, I'm really sorry about last night. My parents just didn't understand. To them, college is practically the most important part of a person's life."

"Not everyone goes to college, Leah. It's not a crime to need to earn a living."

"I know that. They know it too. It's just . . . well, what do you expect from a couple of professors?"

"Don't push it all off on them," Miguel said irritably. "You looked at least as shocked as they did."

"Well . . . maybe I was," she admitted reluctantly. "It's just that you're so smart, Miguel, and it seems like such a waste. I know money is tight for your family now, but there are so many programs . . . I guess I assumed you'd take advantage of one."

"I'm tired of taking advantage! Can't you understand that? When my father was alive, we never took anything off anyone."

"I know, but—"

"No, you *don't* know. We lived in a regular house. We had regular lives. And my dad had his own contracting business. No one gives you a business, Leah. My parents put every penny they had into getting my dad launched as a contractor. They knew it was a risk, but my dad was so sure it would pay off in the end, when the company got big."

He smiled, but it was an angry, bitter smile. "I was headed for college in those days, all right. I was going to study business and work beside my dad. And I'll tell you something: We would have paid for my education *ourselves*, and for Rosa's, too. It was the big American dream. It was the reason my dad worked so hard. . . . It was the reason there wasn't any health insurance when he got sick."

"I'm so sorry," Leah murmured. "Miguel, I wish you would have told me before."

"When Dad died, Mom lost nearly everything paying for the doctors, the funeral. . . . There was no way to keep the business running without Dad, no way to keep the house. But we didn't give up. Mom kept her job. We rented an apartment. We held on like that until her kidneys failed. Then there were more bills, and more, and more."

Leah nodded mutely.

"Now it's all Medicare and Medicaid and public assistance." He suddenly sat up straighter, his expression determined. "But that's about to change. I'd be working already if I hadn't promised my father I'd finish school."

"I don't believe your mother would let you drop out."

Miguel made a face. "She doesn't even want me to work, except in the summer. She says I can't bring in enough to change things, and that I should enjoy my high school years."

Leah's eyes met Miguel's. They both smiled a little.

"Yeah. Right," they said in unison.

"So that's why I'm not going to college," he concluded. "I can't help it if your parents don't like me because of it."

"They don't dislike you, Miguel."

"Well, they look down on me, then."

"That's because they don't know *why* you're not going. Let me tell them what you just told me, and I promise their attitudes will change. If anything, they'll look up to you instead."

Miguel scowled, then drew a deep breath and shrugged.

Leah decided to interpret that as permission. She hugged him hard and kissed his cheek. "I love you," she whispered against his ear.

Miguel glanced toward the kitchen in alarm. Then, seeing they were unobserved, he kissed her back. "You too," he murmured.

"So, are we okay? Will you call me later?"

"Later? Where are you going now?"

"My mom only let me have her car for an hour. I've got to get back before dinner."

Miguel sighed. "I'll walk you out."

Leah called good-bye to Rosa and Mrs. del Rios; then Miguel opened the front door and the two of them headed down the walkway.

"Where did you park?" he asked, perplexed when he saw no car behind his at the curb.

"Oh, uh, over there." Leah pointed.

"Over where?"

And there was something in his voice that made her heart start pounding.

She glanced at her mother's white hatchback and realized she'd done a stupid thing. She could have parked nearly anywhere, but for some reason she'd parked in the exact same spot she'd taken the morning she'd spied on him.

"That's your car?" he asked, his face expressionless.

"Well, my mom's," she admitted, just that moment realizing he'd only ever seen her father's.

"You want to tell me what you were doing parked there a couple of weeks ago?" he asked angrily. "I saw some weirdo sitting over there, trying to hide, but I never guessed it was you!"

"It, uh, are you sure that—"

"I wrote down the license plate, Leah. Want me to go get it?"

"You did?" she asked weakly.

"Wouldn't you, if some psycho was parked in your neighborhood? I didn't know what the heck was going on. What *was* going on?"

"Oh, Miguel, I'm so sorry," she said, beginning to cry with shame and remorse. "I only wanted to see where you lived. I just wanted to know what you did on the weekends."

"How did you get my address?"

"I followed you home from school," she admitted tearfully.

"On a Saturday?"

"No, a different day. And then I came back on Saturday to see what you were doing. I followed you on your errands. I'm so sorry. I feel like such a fool. And I wanted to tell you, but—"

"You were afraid I might be mad?" Miguel's voice was loud and sarcastic, and his tan cheeks were ruddy with anger. "Why would I be mad, Leah? Because you went behind my back? Because you totally invaded my privacy? Or maybe because you lied about not knowing where I lived. Maybe—"

"Please, Miguel," she begged, crying harder. She reached for his hand, but he jerked it away. "I *wanted* to tell you," she pleaded. "I'm sor—"

"You know what? Forget it. Save your apologies for someone who cares. This isn't working out, Leah. It never has, and it never will."

"No! Miguel, that's not true."

"Why don't you run on home to your snobby parents and find some nice, safe college boy to make them happy? I don't want to see you anymore."

"Miguel!" She was crying so hard she could barely say his name. "Please don't. Don't make—"

Behind them, Miguel's front door was thrown open so suddenly and with so much force that Leah stopped in the middle of her thought. She caught only a glimpse of Rosa, who was flushed an unnatural shade of pink, before she ducked her head to hide her streaming eyes.

"Miguel! Miguel!" Rosa screamed, loudly enough for the entire street to hear. "Dr. Gibson just called, and they have a kidney for Mom!"